ALADDIN AND THE FLYING DUTCHMAN

ALADDIN AND THE FLYING DUTCHMAN

THE ALADDIN TRILOGY #3

J. R. RAIN

PIERS ANTHONY

ACCLAIM FOR J.R. RAIN AND PIERS ANTHONY:

"Anthony's most ambitious project to date. Well conceived and written from the heart."
—**Library Journal** on Piers Anthony's *Isle of Woman*

"Be prepared to lose sleep!"
—**James Rollins**, international bestselling author of *The Doomsday Key*

"Piers Anthony is a writer of passion. *Volk* is a masterpiece."
—**Brad Linaweaver**, author of *Moon of Ice*

"*Dark Horse* is the best book I've read in a long time!"
—**Gemma Halliday**, award-winning author of *Spying in High Heels*

"Piers Anthony is one of the more colorful personalities in the SF world."
—***Science Fiction Chronicle*** on Piers Anthony's *Bio of an Ogre*

"*Moon Dance* is a must read. If you like Janet Evanovich's Stephanie Plum, bounty hunter, be prepared to love J.R. Rain's Samantha Moon, vampire private investigator."
—**Eve Paludan**, author of *Letters from David*

OTHER BOOKS BY PIERS ANTHONY AND J.R. RAIN

STANDALONE NOVELS
Dragon Assassin
Dolfin Tayle
Jack and the Giants

THE ALADDIN TRILOGY
Aladdin Relighted
Aladdin Sins Bad
Aladdin and the Flying Dutchman

ISBN: 1500676330

ISBN 13: 9781500676339

ACKNOWLEDGMENTS

A special thank you to Rudy Reyes and Sandy Johnston.

CHAPTER ONE

We sailed high above Djinnland.

From up here, I had a new appreciation for this magical landscape, which was far more beautiful than I had realized. Perhaps the removal of the cancer, Prince Zeyn, had something to do with it. Indeed, the land almost seemed to grow more beautiful, more colorful, more alive as we continued to traverse over it.

Sinbad the Sailor was, apparently, a master of all vessels, even magical ones. Granted, he had a ghostly crew to aid him, but he surely seemed comfortable behind the great wheel as he sailed us toward the ball of light in the sky. The ball of light was, of course, the portal into the mortal realms.

The ship itself seemed impervious to the density of Djinnland, or perhaps it just magically made adjustments to it. Either way, we moved swiftly through clouds and past flocks of tiny, fire-breathing dragons.

As the wind hit our faces and the music played on, with my beautiful—and pregnant—wife Jewel cradled in my arms, I got another frantic message from Sylvie the Siren, the sexy sea nymph who was currently in the form of a ring around my index finger.

My lord, we must hurry… my sisters cannot hold the beast back for long.

Her words, as usual, appeared directly in my thoughts, as if spoken just inside my inner ear. Truly, she was a magical creature.

The beast? I asked, framing my question as a thought. I was well accustomed to such communication by now. *What manner of beast?*

Sire, it is unlike anything we've ever seen before.

Although I didn't approve of the mischief caused by the Sirens and their ways—namely, luring sailors and ships to their ultimate demise—I did like Sylvie the Siren, who had proven to be a valuable friend and ally.

Mischief, perhaps, said Sylvie, picking up on my thoughts, which I had not bothered to shield. *But we are also guardians of something of great importance.*

And what is that?

It is a relic, my lord. Obtained from a merchant's ship long ago. We recognized it immediately for what it was and have been guarding it ever since. Perhaps too zealously.

And this relic is why you and your kind lure ships and men to their untimely death?

Partly, my lord. We also love to sing. We cannot help if our voices are accursed.

I knew something of their accursed voices. In fact, I had heard Sylvie herself sing, and it was a haunting sound that I would not soon forget, perhaps never. A part of me always longed to hear it again. But to do so, I knew, meant to forever fall under its spell. I was the rare mortal who was able to break the spell, and that was with the help of my stepson, Duban, a powerful young wizard who preferred to play the flute and lyre.

Fine, I thought. *And what is this relic?*

The Key to Hades, sire.

I grunted. I'd heard about the key, of course, which supposedly unlocked the Gates of Hades, thus giving the owner dominion over not only all demons of hell, but all manner of foul beings locked away for all eternity, as well. The key could literally unleash hell on earth.

And what do you know of this key, Queen Nylon? I asked, addressing the other magical ring on my hand. Yes, two magical rings and two beautiful nymphs. A man should be so cursed.

We are well aware of the key, sire, and the role the Sirens have played in protecting it. In the wrong hands, the world as we know it would cease to exist.

Below, an undulating hillside swept as far as the eye could see, dotted with plump cow-like creatures and stunted trees that blossomed golden leaves that reflected the sun brightly. Or whatever passed for a sun in this world.

Very well, I said. *I shall do my best. I am but one man.*

With a magical ship, said Queen Nylon. *Captained by none other than Sinbad the Sailor.*

"You look concerned, my love?" said Jewel, running her long fingers through my hair the way she did, sending a shivery thrill through me.

I caught her up to date with my conversation with Sylvie and Queen Nylon.

"And this monster is seeking the key to Hell?"

"That I do not know," I said.

"There's never a dull moment with Aladdin of the Lamp." Jewel rubbed her growing belly. "Here's hoping our little one grows up to be a scholar."

"Or a baker," I said, grinning.

I next informed Sinbad of our change in plans. The handsome man, who stood at the helm of the magical ship like a natural, took the news in stride. Indeed, he was an adventurer through and through.

"I have dealt with my share of sea monsters, my friend. Tell the Sirens to fear not, for Sinbad and Aladdin are on their way."

"Or rather," I said good-naturedly, "Aladdin and Sinbad."

"As you wish, sire," he said giving me a mock bow.

Truth was, had my own wife not found the roguish sailor so damn intriguing, I might have let my jealousy go. But, for now, it remained just below the surface, gnawing at me.

Soon a line of rocky crags appeared on the horizon. I pointed to a gap in the rock wall, directly beneath the sun. The ship seemed to be gaining speed. Our hair and clothing whipped about. Then we plunged through the gap, and found ourselves sailing safely over the arching, crumbling bridge that connected the two worlds. And just as we reached the midway point over the bridge—no doubt the point that magically separated the two worlds—the ship lurched slightly, adjusting to the lesser gravitational force of the mortal realms. A magical ship, indeed!

Sinbad nodded to our fellow shipmates, those we had saved from Prince Zeyn's dungeons. They were a merry group, reveling in their freedom, dancing and playing music with my gifted stepson, Duban.

"And what do we do with them, my lord? We can't very well offer them freedom one moment and then thrust them into a dangerous situation the next."

I pondered. According to Sylvie, the Sirens did not have much time. Landing and releasing the freed prisoners would take time. As I thought about it, I saw something curious hanging just below the railing of the ship. Small dhows. Life rafts. Even more curious, they appeared to magically hover along the ship's hull, with no straps or ropes. In fact, there was nothing holding them in place. I pointed them out.

"Aye, my liege," said Sinbad. "Magical dhows. This could be our answer."

With no time to spare, I gathered the others together and warned them of the imminent danger. All those who wanted to escape now with their lives, were free to do so on the magical dhows. All those who wished to stay and fight were more than welcome to do so.

I was more than pleased when many of the men chose to fight. I did not fault the others. Perhaps most surprising was that the Thief of Baghdad chose to stay. I secretly wondered what the famed rascal was angling at.

At any rate, the others we collected in the magical dhows, along with their share of the treasure in the hold. Shortly, the smaller vessels pealed away from the ship's hull, and sped quickly to the land far below. I wished them well.

Soon, the rolling land turned to choppy swells, and when we were many leagues out to sea, the magical dhows returned to us, empty, and reattached themselves to the hull.

4

Shortly, my talented stepson, Duban, came to my side at the ship's railing. His dark hair was mussed and his chubby cheeks were red, no doubt, from the wind. "We are in grave danger, father."

"And when are we not?" I asked, chuckling.

"She is very powerful."

"The great beast?"

"No, father. She who controls the great beast."

"And who is that?"

Duban shook his head grimly, his brown eyes reflecting the blue sea and skies beyond. "Her magic is too great for me to penetrate."

Too great for Duban? A lad who had been prophesied to be the next great wizard? My lightheartedness abated in an instant. What manner of creature awaited us?

The seas turned choppy again, and I soon saw the reason why: a great creature churned the water, a creature unlike anything I had ever seen. It was the size of a small land mass, with many great tentacles that seemed to reach everywhere at once. Never had I seen anything like it before.

At the ship's wheel, Sinbad stared in amazement. Indeed, all of us stared in amazement. No doubt those who had decided to stay and fight were now regretting their decision.

Hell, *I* was regretting my decision.

Cursing under my breath, I next saw a merchant's ship not too far away, rocking on the churning sea. A lone figure stood on the deck, calmly watching the horrific scene.

Sinbad soon joined me at the railing. "It is as I feared," he said. "The only other creature that could foreseeably threaten the Siren stronghold."

"What is it?" I asked, staring down at the monstrosity that appeared to be part octopus, part squid, all nightmare.

"A kraken. The greatest of all monsters, on sea or on land. We are in for a rough time of it, my liege."

Queen Nylon's words appeared urgently in my thoughts: *My lord, a kraken can only be commanded to attack. Normally they are peaceful creatures who exist in the deepest oceans. Unless they are called forth to do evil.*

I nodded and looked again at the figure standing calmly on the merchant ship. Was this the person responsible for the attack?

Sylvie's words next appeared: *My lord, my sisters are dying. Please, we must hurry!*

Indeed, I could see the other Sirens now, circling the great creature, looking minuscule in comparison. Great tentacles splashed down, no doubt killing the Sirens in an instant.

I gripped the ship's railing. We had to do something.

But what?

CHAPTER TWO

As I stood there with my mind locking up, as it sometimes does when I'm under tension, I suffered a frustratingly irrelevant recent memory. I tried to banish it, as it was only interfering with the present issue.

No, let it flow, Nylon thought.

But we can't afford to waste time on foolishness, I protested.

Trust me. I have a notion how men's foolish minds work. There may be something here.

She was kind to put it that way. But since I had nothing better to offer at the moment, I indulged her. I let the memory flow. Fortunately it was a brief one. It concerned our exploration of the Flying Dutchman's hold while the ship was at bay in Djinnland. It seemed that while the main hold was filled with gold, at least until the crewmen left, there was a smaller hold that retained some of the original cargo. Jewel had explored it, and discovered what appeared to be a bottle of perfume. She had brought it to me. "May I take this?" she inquired in a tone that suggested that I could give only one answer.

"Let me see it," I said, curious myself. I took the bottle and held it up to the light. It seemed almost to glow with an inner urgency.

Beware, Sylvie warned. She was on the hand that held the bottle. *There's a curse on it.*

"A curse?" I repeated somewhat stupidly.

"What are you muttering about?" Jewel demanded. "That's a perfectly good bottle of Lovers' Desperation perfume, a wonderfully rare vintage. It must have been there for a long time. Who else on this ship would have a use for it?"

"Sylvie says it's cursed."

It is, Sylvie thought. *We sirens know a good curse when we smell one. Ask Nylon.*

I moved the bottle to the other hand. "Queen Nylon," I said aloud so Jewel could participate. "Sylvie says this is cursed."

She's right, Nylon agreed immediately. *That hold must have been missed when the ship was decontaminated, so the original curse remains on its artifacts. Do not open it.*

"She confirms the curse," I told Jewel. "You should not use this stuff."

"I think the concubines are just jealous because they have no use for quality perfume," Jewel said, taking the bottle from my hand. "I have no superstitious fear of old worn-out curses."

"These are not mere concubines," I reminded her. "They are supernatural creatures who know something about magic. I think we had best proceed with caution. Maybe Duban can nullify the curse."

"Pshaw," she snorted. Then, before I could protest further, she popped the ancient cork, inverted the bottle, and let a single viscous drop of substance land on her hand. She recorked the bottle and touched the perfume behind either ear. "This will truly bring out the real me," she said, satisfied. "I'll make a phenomenal impression on every man in range." As if she needed to impress anyone except me. But I knew better than to speak that thought aloud.

You're learning, Nylon thought, amused.

For a moment it was like a frozen tableau as we waited for anything to happen. Nothing did. So maybe it wasn't much of a curse. But then there came a whiff of the stench of rotten eggs soaked in septic sewage and allowed to ripen beyond their time. Jewel wrinkled her nose.

"Must be the smell of the monster," I said, looking around.

But no one else seemed to notice it. Until a gust of wind passed us. Then the sailors downwind suddenly gasped and coughed, turning slightly green.

"Uh-oh," I murmured.

It's the perfume, Sylvie thought, picking up the stink from my nostrils.

The cursed perfume, Nylon agreed.

"Uh, Jewel—" I started.

But she was already sniffing the air around her. "Ugh!" She ran to a bucket of slops, the closest available liquid, and dipped out gobs to splash behind her ears. But it seemed only to enhance the effect.

Mortals don't listen well, Nylon noted with a faint aura of I-told-you-so.

That's their curse, Sylvie agreed with just the hint of a mental smirk.

I went to help Jewel wash, keeping my mouth shut for more than one reason. Soon we were in our cabin and she was in a tub as I doused her with buckets of sea water. In due course she was bedraggled but odor-free, while the tub, to put it politely, stank to the lofty welkin. We got Jewel into new clothing and locked the cabin door, sealing off the festering tubful. What a putrid mess! We took a new cabin, as it might be weeks before the old one was sanitary.

I said nothing further, knowing what was good for me. The stoppered bottle was returned to the hold. That was the end of it. After that, we had begun our journey home.

Until this moment, as the memory ran its course. "So what has this to do with the price of beans in Bohemia?" I subvocally asked Queen Nylon. Because I was still on the spot to deal with the monstrous kraken, and still unable to think of anything. If I didn't come up with something fast it would be bad for my reputation, not to mention my body, as the tentacles discovered the ship.

Silly, that's the answer, she responded. *The kraken has a very fine sense of smell, or more properly, taste.*

"So?" I saw no connection.

She had mercy on me. *Give the monster a taste of perfume.*

Then it burst upon me. The curse! If that stuff tasted as bad to the kraken as it smelled to us, it would be like a mythical stench bomb.

"I think the kraken is a lady," I said aloud. "We should honor her with a libation."

"What are you mumbling nonsensically about now?" Jewel asked with her usual appreciation for my powers of intellect.

"It's a water predator," I explained condescendingly. "It tastes the water to zero in on its prey. It must be pretty sensitive to locate quarry thousands of leagues away."

"So?" She saw no connection.

"We shall give the kraken a taste of cursed perfume. That may prove to be a distraction."

"Perfume!" Then it came to her. "The vilest stench!"

"The same," I agreed pleasantly. "Starting with the more dilute version, which we need to dispose of anyway." I turned to the nearest sailors. "Men, haul the tub out of the cabin." I signaled Sinbad. "Take the ship right up beside the kraken."

"Beside the monster?" Sinbad exclaimed. "This is suicide!"

"No, it is honoring a lady," Jewel said.

Sinbad gave her a look that said "So?" but did not admit that he made no sense of this.

The crewmen grumbled between choking fits, but got the roiling tub out on deck. Sinbad also grumbled, but guided the ship out over the shallow edge of the monster. They all seemed to feel that I had lost my idiotic mind, but I was the one in charge, so my folly had to be indulged.

Tentacles were reaching up the sides of the ship, seeking holds.

Then I had the crewmen dump the tub onto the back of the kraken. We could see the foul liquid bubbling as it spread across the flesh. "Now move off," I called to Sinbad. "Quickly."

He was more than glad to oblige. The ship broke free of the grasping tentacles and sluiced away from the monster.

The kraken seemed to have a problem. UGH! it honked, just as if it smelled something bad. Its myriad tentacles churned the surrounding water. But that seemed only to spread the stink further. It seemed that the cursed perfume was marvelously intense, so that diluting it merely amplified the taste.

We watched. Jewel was actually smiling.

The kraken sounded. It descended in the water so rapidly that a whirlpool formed above it. That vortex caught the ship and sought to drag it into the swirling center. That was mischief.

But I knew what to do. "Duban," I said. "If you happen to have a wind spell handy..."

Duban worked his magic. A stiff breeze came up, blowing away from the whirlpool. Sinbad quickly accommodated the ship, and soon it was riding before the wind, escaping the whirlpool. We were safe.

"Good thinking, dad," Duban said. "Wind is easy; it was the monster that was beyond me."

"Of course, son," I agreed patronizingly. "That's why I stepped in."

Jewel shot me a look of mixed disgust and admiration. She knew I had lucked out, this time, and surely suspected that I had done so with the help of the women I had wrapped around my fingers.

We'll never tell, Nylon thought, amused again.

Women do this sort of thing for men all the time, Sylvie agreed. But I felt her quickly turn somber.

You are concerned for your sister sirens? I subvocalized and thought to her.

Yes, sire. My sisters need my help. We have suffered much loss today.

Go to them. Hurry.

Thank you, sire!

And with that, she rapidly uncurled from my finger and transformed to her proper size and shape. Now naked and jaw-droppingly beautiful, she bowed to me slightly, then leaped over the railing. Once in the water, her feet instantly transformed into a tail. She thrust once, twice, and soon disappeared from sight. Indeed, there was a great wailing from the ocean, but these were not the haunting Sirens' call. These were songs of mourning, and I felt for the magical creatures.

"What of the other ship?" Sinbad said to me when Sylvie was gone.

The merchanter! I had quite forgotten it in my need to deal with the kraken. It had been blown clear of the whirlpool by the same wind that saved us. Now it was within hailing distance, and the person remained on its deck.

As I squinted to make it out, I saw that the figure was female, and quite attractive, especially with the wind blowing against her garment and drawing on her long hair. Who was she, and why had she seemed so unafraid of the doom that had threatened her? Or was my first thought accurate, that she might actually have brought the monster here? In that case she might be dangerous. How could we know?

"Hail the ship," I told Sinbad. "We need to learn more about it, before we join the sirens." As if this were a routine interaction.

"She's beautiful," Jewel said. "Unfortunately you don't need another concubine."

Amen to that, Nylon agreed. *A man sees a shapely outline, and whatever common sense he might have dissipates into lust.*

She was in a position to know. Sometimes there seemed to be too many women surrounding me. It hampered my style.

CHAPTER THREE

J ust as Sinbad turned the great wheel in preparation for contact with the errant ship, a dense fog rolled in. So dense and so sudden, that I sensed sorcery.

The small merchant ship was immediately enshrouded in fog. So much so, that it disappeared from sight.

"Duban," I murmured.

The boy twitched his fingers, and the fog thinned. Routine minor magic, for him, like practicing his scales. The ship dimly reappeared.

In that instant, Sylvie Siren leaped from the sea, transformed in mid-air, and landed on the deck with human feet. Truly a remarkable magical feat.

"It is gone, Aladdin," she cried out.

"What is gone?"

"The Key to Hades."

"But I don't understand, we stopped the kraken—"

"Which only served as a diversion. The thief had struck even while the great beast attacked my sister sirens. Three are dead."

"Blast. But who could pull off such an outrageous—"

And it struck me. Of course, I knew of a thief skilled enough; indeed, the one thief who had already penetrated the bowels of the Sirens' lair.

The Thief of Baghdad.

As Sylvie returned to my finger, I ordered Sinbad and the others to search for the thief, but the wretch, of course, was nowhere to be found. Cursing, I next turned my attention to the nearby merchant vessel, which was clarifying as we approached it, and soon grappling lines were sent out, latching the merchanter to our own. Sinbad and a handful of men boarded the smaller ship. To my surprise, the young woman, who only looked more beautiful the closer we got, threw herself into the stunned sailor's arms.

Shortly, she was led aboard the *Dutchman* and over to me, where I stood with my wife, Duban, and Nydea Nymph, who was presently betrothed to Sinbad. Our newest passenger, the girl, explained that she was to be fed to the kraken, as a reward for its services. Indeed, nine others, equally young and fair, had already been consumed by the great beast.

"I was the last, my lord. The final, choice meal. I had watched in horror as the previous nine were rendered in half and shoved into the monster's hideous maw."

I shuddered. Now I understood why she had thrown herself into Sinbad's arms! She must have been frozen in horror, watching the kraken, rather than nonchalant. "And who did this to you?" I asked. "Who submitted you to such brutality?"

"We never saw him," she said, shuddering. "But he was surely a consummately evil man, with power we could not deny."

Beware, Nylon thought. *It is too easy to blame an anonymous male. Be polite, but do not trust her yet.*

Good advice. "Feed this girl," I said to one of the human crew. "And make sure she has clean clothing and a warm bed."

"Aye, my lord."

But instead of going with them, she threw herself at my feet, in the process revealing new aspects of her body, especially her full bosom. "Thank you, my lord! You are wonderful!"

That view is deliberate, Nylon thought. *She's a pro.*

As a ruler, I am not unfamiliar with having someone throw themselves at my feet. Generally, though, I know the reason. Here, I was as stunned as anyone. "Get back on your feet," I said, stalling for a bit of time.

She got slowly and gracefully to her feet, her limber body displaying itself even more impressively as she did.

A pro, Nylon repeated.

My wife's initial assessment was true: the woman was indeed beautiful. But now that I was close-up, I could appreciate just how beautiful: long, dark hair, almond-shaped eyes, slender neck and full lips. Her lashes, I noted, were impossibly long. Perhaps the longest I'd ever seen.

"What's your name?" I asked, finding speaking suddenly difficult. Jewel, I noted, was watching my reaction very carefully, curiously. She sensed something was amiss, obviously. Behind me, the other men on board gathered, like seabirds around entrails.

Men, said Nylon. *So predictable.*

"I am called Dea." She smiled shyly and held my gaze long enough for me to eventually look away. I suddenly felt like a young ruffian with his first crush.

The men all quickly agreed that this was the most beautiful name they had ever heard. Sinbad, too. Even Duban nodded along. A pro indeed!

"Oh, brother," said Jewel. Evidently, the maiden's charms were lost on my wife—and the women on board.

I said to the woman, "From which port do you hail? We shall return you to your home."

"I do not know, master."

"You don't know?"

"I have been a slave all my life. At sea all my life."

"A slave?" I asked, surprised. She did not have the appearance of a slave. If anything—

"A sex slave, master," she said, confirming my suspicions. "A *prized* sex slave."

That I could believe. I swallowed hard and suddenly found speaking difficult again. Not that I approved of sex slaves; in fact, slavery of any type was something I was working hard to abolish from my kingdom. But Dea actually sounded as if she…enjoyed being used by the crew. The men around me sensed it as well, and now there was a great chattering behind me, sounding much like the monkeys in my royal zoo.

I found my tongue again, which seemed to have gotten stuck to the roof of my mouth. I cleared my throat with difficulty. "I'm sorry to hear that, Dea. You're safe here."

"You are my hero." She turned and looked at the surrounding, stupefied men. "All of you."

The men beamed and puffed out their chests, and my wife had evidently seen enough. She banished all of them, shaking her head. "Pathetic," she said, as the men reluctantly moved off. She turned to Dea. "I believe you to be a witch."

"That is a hurtful thing to say, mistress. I am but a simple slave."

"Yes, a sex slave. You've made that abundantly clear." My wife next leaned into me and spoke into my ear: "It's not becoming for a king to drool over himself."

Then she took the girl's hand and led her away. Nydea Nymph followed, and I heard my wife tell the girl they would give her a bath and clean her up.

"She is a healthy one," said Sinbad, as we watched the trio depart.

"Aye."

"So where to now, Aladdin?"

As I considered our options, Sylvie spoke up. *Sire, we sirens could use the cursed perfume, should we cross paths again with the kraken. It proved more than effective. We have, of course the original, uncursed perfume.*

Would be a nice gesture for Jewel, said Nylon. *Seeing that you ticked her off.*

Will I ever do anything right? I asked.

Are you a male? asked Sylvie, and she giggled.

"A barter, then," I said aloud, in which case Sinbad looked at me curiously, then went back to the helm. He was getting used to such strange outbursts from me, knowing I was guided by the two nymphs.

Shortly, the exchange was made, with Sylvie acting as the go-between, and soon I was presented with an elegant bottle of what appeared to be the exact perfume. I unstoppered the bottle and gave it a sniff. Heavenly.

Jewel will be pleased, said Nylon. *Unless, of course, you fail to keep your hands off the new slave.*

The Siren queen has a message for you, Aladdin, said Sylvie.

And what is that?

To find the key at all costs.

I thought you might say that. Does she have a suggestion as to where to begin?

The key is undoubtedly on its way to its final destination.

How is this possible? I said, perplexed. *Where could the key have gone? We are the only ship out here.*

Look again, my lord.

I did look, and I saw what she was referring to. The small merchanter, once tethered to the *Dutchman*, was gone.

But how?

A cloaking spell, no doubt.

Fine, I said, grumbling. *And where does the queen suggest we look for the key?*

The Gates of Hades are located in the Hinterland.

The Hinterland? And where is that?

It is a forbidden mountain range deep in the heart of the Sahara.

So be it. I turned to Sinbad. "Plot us a course due west."

"Due west?"

I told him about my conversation with Sylvie Siren, and Sinbad, always on the lookout for a good adventure, grinned broadly. "West it is!"

He next gave the order and the ghostly crew responded instantly, many appearing as if from thin air, their bodies nearly invisible in the bright sunshine. Sails were hoisted, lines were drawn, and soon the ship was cutting sharply through the water, faster than any other ship.

Supernaturally fast, I knew.

Soon the rocky coast of the African continent appeared and Sinbad gave another order and the ship majestically rose out of the sea, and into the blue sky.

And over the Dark Continent.

CHAPTER FOUR

It was fine, for a while. I gazed at the mountains and valleys below, lost in the wonder of the landscape. I had not been to the Dark Continent before, and this was a superlative view.

Duban and his fiancee Myrrh came to join me. Well, technically she was only his girlfriend, as he was thirteen and she twelve and I did not support child marriages, and Duban had not made an official arrangement with her, but she would marry him in due course. She had foreseen it, and she had some future vision along with her telepathy. Regardless, she was a fine and pretty girl, slender, dark-eyed, and with long lustrous black hair. I could not have selected a better match for my son.

Thank you, Aladdin.

I almost jumped, while Sylvie and Nylon laughed. *Forget she could read your mind?* Nylon teased me.

I was mainly relieved that I hadn't been thinking anything bad about Myrrh, given that I might as well have been speaking my mind aloud. Not that there was anything bad to think of.

"Thank you," Myrrh repeated aloud with the hint of a smile.

Though sometimes maybe she deserved to be spanked.

Nu-uh, Nylon thought. *You may spank* my *plush bare bottom when I resume full natural form, but she's too young for such attention.*

"Not by much," Myrrh murmured, looking straight ahead.

Oops. Now it was Nylon's turn to be embarrassed. Myrrh could read her mind too, and, thanks to her telepathy, was well familiar with the dubious joys of adult interaction.

19

"What is much?" Duban asked. He had been left out of this dialogue, fortunately.

"I was thinking Myrrh is too young to be so pretty," I said quickly. "She read my mind. But she doesn't like to be patronized. And she's right: she is almost a woman."

"And I'm still a child?" he asked, annoyed.

How sensitive could you get? "You are almost a man."

"And I don't like to be patronized either," he retorted.

Myrrh took his hand. "Aladdin means well," she said.

I could see Duban melting. Myrrh could handle him without even trying.

"Kings do," Duban agreed reluctantly. He still had not completely accepted my relationship with his mother, though that was what made him a prince.

"We came to you for another purpose," Myrrh said to me. "It's about Dea."

"The slave girl," I agreed noncommittally, seeing a mental picture of her considerable physical charms. Jewel said I didn't need another concubine, but really, could a man ever have too many concubines? She would be a tempting addition.

"She is more than a slave girl," Duban said. "There is an aura of power about her that I can't fathom. I distrust that."

"And I can't read her mind," Myrrh said. "It is as if there is a patch of fog about her that shrouds her thoughts. I don't trust that."

"We believe you should stay away from her," Duban said.

"So does your mother," I said. "But really, what would be the harm? It isn't as if a man needs to appreciate a woman's mind. She's a sex slave!"

"She's dangerous," Myrrh said. "Until we know more about her, you should remain clear."

I sighed. Jewel had a slightly jealous nature, even during her pregnancy, but Duban and Myrrh were genuinely trying to help me. Their warning had to be taken seriously. "I will remain clear," I said with regret.

Then we focused on the landscape below the ship. I noticed something new. There was a kind of rough channel through the mountains, many of which were volcanoes, extending from horizon to horizon. It was almost as if the very rock had cracked to form a chasm. Was I imagining a pattern where none existed?

Some day they will call it the Rift Valley, Nylon thought. *Where some nether demon pushed the mountains apart. Those demons are constantly playing their games, showing their power.*

"Oh, thank you," I said. I would not have credited it, but Nylon had been around the past and the future, and could be right.

We flew on to a great desert. *The Sahara,* Nylon thought. *Once there were rivers there, but there came a drought.*

It must have been some dry spell! The desert extended as far as I could see.

Then there came an adverse wind, a hot draft blowing from the desert, trying to push us back the way we came. "We'll have to tack," Sinbad called. "Slanting into the wind, back and forth. That will slow progress."

I knew about tacking. Winds were capricious, and this was a sailing ship, even if it was airborne at the moment. It was propelled by the wind. "So be it," I agreed.

Another person approached us. It was Dea, looking remarkably sexy as the wind hauled at her hair and flattened her clothing against her body. I thought nothing could be more impressive than bare breasts, but somehow her wind-pressed bosom was more so. "Lord Aladdin!" she called. "I fear the wind will blow me away. You must hold me."

She couldn't think of a better line than that? Nylon thought, disgusted.

"Don't do it," Duban and Myrrh said almost together.

"We'll all go to our cabins," I said, avoiding the issue.

"I must be with you!" Dea said.

"You will be safer with the women," I said, realizing that could be taken more than one way. I retreated hastily to my own cabin, leaving her behind though I would have much preferred holding her as she wished. Was greater sacrifice ever required of a man?

The winds buffeted us as the ship tacked into them. Sinbad knew what he was doing, but this was really rough weather. We might do better to land and anchor until the storm passed.

No, we'd be buried in brush, Nylon thought. *Would you like me to emulate your wife and distract you for an hour?*

That was tempting, but this buffeting was making me too nervous. "Some other time," I muttered.

Then it got worse. I peered out, and got smote by a face full of flying sand. What was happening?

Sandstorm, Nylon thought. *They happen in the desert.*

"A storm made of sand?" I asked, bemused.

Yes, in essence. The winds pick up the sand and blow it about. It's a perfectly natural occurrence.

Natural! Not in my experience. But of course I had not been to Africa before.

Wor-sand-worse, Sylvie thought, mentally spelling it out to be sure my dull mind would get the pun.

"We can't fight it," Sinbad called. "We'll have to ride with it."

Oh? What had we been doing up till now? I was beginning to feel sea sick.

Maybe you should eat a sand witch, Nylon thought mischievously.

Eat? That did it. I barely grabbed a bucket in time to catch my heave.

Your sandy humor sickens him, Sylvie thought.

Forget Myrrh. Both these nymphs needed spanking.

Both caught that thought, and sent out pictures of their shapely bare backsides, inviting me to have at them. Knowing I was too sick at the moment to do anything even if I had the chance. They were consummate teases.

But soon the ship straightened out and flew with the wind. That enabled me to recover.

We went out on deck. The wind remained strong, but now the sand storm was harmlessly behind us. We were cruising over the Rift Valley, as Nylon called it.

Legend has it that the Garden of Eden is in this vicinity, Nylon thought. *After Adam and Eve were booted, Allah filled it in with water so there could be no return.*

"What legend is this?" I demanded truculently. The Nymph was taking this whole business far too lightly.

Oh, just a tidbit I picked up from here or there.

Jewel, Dea, Duban, and Myrrh emerged from their cabins. Dea headed for me, but Duban and Myrrh blocked her off. "Is this the way to the Hinterland?" Jewel asked.

"Sinbad shifted course to avoid the sand storm," I explained.

"But we have left that far behind. Why are we still going south?"

Good question. "Time to change course?" I called to Sinbad.

"I'm trying to!" Sinbad called back. "The ship's not responding." Indeed, the ghost sailors were hard at work, but their efforts were having no apparent effect.

Something was moving the ship south against our wishes. I did not like the feel of this.

Then a body of water came into sight. It was a great lake. The Dutchman sailed down toward it, and splashed into the water. We had arrived—somewhere.

"Why, it's Eden!" Dea exclaimed, surprised.

"Looks more like a lake to me," Jewel said sourly.

"It's a lake now," Dea said. "But in early times it was the Garden."

"How do you know this?"

"Oh, everyone knows," Dea said. "Allah knew mankind would return to easy living if he had a chance, so he made sure there was no chance. So now it's Lake Defeatia, showing the defeat of foolish Adam."

She's right, Nylon thought. *Perhaps Dea has been around a while.*

"I've got it!" Duban exclaimed. "The Flying Dutchman is an enchanted water ship. It can fly when directed, but prefers water, because flying takes a lot more energy. So when it spies water it naturally goes to it, especially when it's tired. It saw this lake, and went to it. Once it is rested, it will fly again."

"How do you know this?" Dea asked him.

Duban almost smiled. "Everyone knows the legends. I just had to remember the right one for the occasion."

Dea nodded slowly. It was almost as if she remembered this legend too, but did not care to say so. The woman *had* been around. More than she wanted us to know.

All things considered, it seemed best to rest on the lake for a day or so, letting the ship recover. That sand storm must have worn it out.

CHAPTER FIVE

Sinbad appeared with one of the ship's original crew. The ghost rose and fell on ethereal currents as he held the faint wisps of his hands together nervously. Who knew a ghost could be nervous? There was the faint remains of a wound just under his jaw. Surely a fatal wound which directly led to his current departed state.

"Aladdin, this specter wishes to speak with you."

"Ghosts can speak?" I asked, surprised.

It was coming on evening, and the ghosts were slightly easier to see in the dimming light. Their ectoplasmic forms seemed to glow from within, lighting up their immediate vicinity with an unearthly light that, quite frankly, I don't think I would ever get used to.

Sinbad shrugged. "Judge for yourself, Aladdin."

The skittish, translucent spirit stepped forward, "Master," he said; or, rather, I *think* he said. His raspy, whispery voice could have just as easily been the desert wind moaning over the deck. I strained to listen as he continued: "The ship is experiencing unexpected difficulties."

"What difficulties?" I asked, realizing that this was perhaps the first time in my life that I'd addressed a ghost directly. By Allah, I live a strange life!

"We are experiencing an unaccounted drag upon the ship."

"Has this ever happened before?"

"Once, when the ship was bewitched."

"Duban," I said, turning to my son. "Do you sense any bewitchment upon this ship?"

The boy nodded and closed his eyes. A moment later, he looked up at me and shook his head. "No, Father. But I do sense...something."

"What?"

"Another," he said guardedly.

"Another what?" I asked.

But the boy only shook his head. "I do not know, Father, but I sense there's more to this than we can see."

I had an idea. "Myrrh?"

"Yes, my liege?"

"Cast your thoughts about the ship. Look for the one known as the Thief of Baghdad."

She nodded. "Aye, sire," she said, already picking up on the ship lingo. She, too, closed her eyes as she turned in a small circle. She nodded. "Yes, sire. He is here."

My jaw dropped. So did Sinbad's. I reached for my scimitar, as did he his own. "Where is that wretch?"

She shook her head. "I only sense his thoughts, sire. I cannot pinpoint."

"Perhaps his thoughts will give him away," said Sinbad. Like me, Sinbad never liked the rascal. Sinbad, like me, saw through his greasy charms.

But Myrrh only shook her head again. "His thoughts are guarded, master Sinbad. Perhaps by magic. I cannot gain entry. I only sense his mind is near."

I looked again at the ghost captain, who was waiting for me patiently, nervously wringing his hands and rising and falling on mysterious winds. I said, "What, then, must we do to accommodate the drag?"

"We can wait until the ship has fully recovered, master."

"And how long will that take?"

"Perhaps another four or five days."

Too long, said Sylvie, speaking urgently. *The Gates of Hades will be opened by then.*

Unless the key is with us, said Queen Nylon. *You heard the young telepath. The thief is near, somehow.*

Unless he gave the key to another, countered Sylvie. *There's more than one way to get to the Hinterlands. Perhaps another had a magic carpet. Or a trained roc. Or a—*

"Quiet," I commanded, sub-vocalizing the word. "Give me a chance to think. Sometimes I think I'm going crazy with you two in my head."

"What about me?" asked Myrrh, teasingly.

I growled under my breath and turned back to the ghost who was still patiently waiting. "Is there any other option?"

"Yes, master," he said eagerly, nodding his ghostly head. "There is indeed another way."

He explained that magic was limitless, and the Flying Dutchman was no different. To keep it aloft required, apparently, an astronomical amount of magic. Magic that needed to be restored periodically. Our flight from Djinnland and now the flight over the desert—with the sandstorm and now this additional, unknown drag—had depleted the ship's supernatural resources.

"I understand," I said. "What do you propose?"

"An outside energy source would be suitable, master."

"What kind of outside energy source?"

"Anything powerful enough to fuel the ship, master."

I rubbed my face, ran my fingers through my thick hair. All eyes were on me, ghostly and humanly alike. What did I know of such enchantments? I didn't, and, out of habit, nearly called upon Lamprey. Surely my powerful djinn could have fueled a hundred such sky ships.

The problem was obvious: how to search for an energy source while presently trapped on a lake? I sensed Sylvie's growing anxiety. The longer we waited, the more likely the devil key was on its way to the Gates of Hades.

To my surprise, Dea the slave girl stepped forward. "Sire, let me remind you that we are presently floating over what some think was once the Garden of Eden."

Sinbad grunted. "A legend only, woman."

"But one that might be true," she persisted.

"And if the legends are true," I said. "What of it?"

She walked over to me and nearly laid a hand on me but, seeing the glare in Jewel's eyes, obviously thought better of it. "The Garden of Eden contains the Tree of Life."

"Again, enlighten me, slave," I said.

"There are a great many power sources on the earth," she said. "Some are natural and others are man-made. A great ring of rock on the emerald isle, pyramids on both sides of the earth, sacred stones and sacred forests. Do you see where I'm going with this, my king?"

"You are saying the Tree of Life is such a power source?"

"No," she said, grinning seductively. "I'm saying that it is, perhaps, the *most* powerful. And it's directly beneath us."

"But the lake is flooded," countered Sinbad.

She spun on him. "Not all of it. The tree is too valuable, too necessary."

"And you know this how?" asked Jewel.

"As a slave, you hear things, especially if your master is particularly powerful."

I thought about this, chewing my lip, noticing that the desert wind had picked up again. The great ship rocked noticeably upon the lake.

As much as it grates me to admit it, said Queen Nylon, *I think the slave might be right. Most of my kind are aware of the Tree of Life and its reputed power. In fact, some say that it's the source of all life on earth.*

Then we must go to it at once, said Sylvie urgently. *I can help guide us to it.*

I thought about this some more, drumming my fingers on a nearby railing. All eyes were still on me. A decision must be made.

"Duban," I said finally.

"Yes, father?"

"Can you fashion a breathing device for myself and two others?"

"Of course, father."

I nodded. "Then we will find the Tree of Life, and return with a suitable power source."

Sylvie squeezed my finger; Dea smiled broadly, almost wickedly. At least two people were happy with my decision.

CHAPTER SIX

Soon Duban had conjured the swimming equipment, which consisted of masks resembling pig snouts—that really bothered me, because pigs are unclean, but I suppressed my aversion, knowing it was misplaced—that covered our mouths and noses, with hoses that entered packs on our backs. I gathered that those packs contained a lot of squeezed air. There were also fishlike fins that we could don as gloves for our hands and slippers for our feet. I knew that these would really help; suddenly I would be able to swim much better than ever before.

"Use some of this," Jewel said, anointing each of us with a drop of fluid. "It will protect you from predators."

"What is it?" I asked.

"Cursed perfume. I saved a little, just in case."

Now I smelled it. It was awful. Maybe she was having revenge for her own humiliation. But she was right: it should drive away hostile creatures.

The three of us splashed into the water. Sylvie detached from my finger and resumed her natural form, swimming ahead of us. I could see Sinbad's eyes goggling as he looked at her flexing bare legs, and Duban's too; I wish she could have worn pantaloons or something. But I suspected that my own eyes were goggling too.

Three crocodiles headed for us—and sheared away before getting close enough to bite. The perfume was working.

Then Sylvie changed her legs into a tail and dived. She had of course been teasing us by leaving her feet on so her legs could flex apart. She angled down into the dark water and disappeared. That was worse; how could we follow her if we could not see her?

I glanced at Duban. He nodded. Then a dim glow appeared, enough to enable us to see in the shadowed recesses. The siren was still descending. We followed. The fins really helped and, of course, this would be impossible without the breathing masks. The hoses must be bringing air in from somewhere else; the backpacks were not big enough to hold the amount we were breathing. But who cared, as long as they worked?

We reached the bottom, which really wasn't far down. It was covered in what resembled seaweed, forming a dark green mat.

And there in the distance before us was a hill, not high enough to become an island, but it had its own colored foliage. It looked a lot like an island, as maybe it once had been. In the center was a mighty tree. That must be the Tree of Life, not bothered by the surrounding water.

A merman with a flaming sword appeared. "Begone, sons of Adam!" he cried. "Your kind is forbidden in these demesnes!"

How did he call out aloud, under water? And why wasn't that sword promptly quenched?

We paused, dismayed. Then I realized. We had forgotten that Allah had posted an angel with a flaming sword to prevent men from returning to the Garden of Eden. The magical blade hardly cared about the water, or the stench of cursed perfume, but was surely quite capable of dismembering us. Did we really want to invoke the wrath of Allah?

Sylvie swam back to me and touched my flippered hand. *I'll handle this*, she thought. *Wait your chance.*

"But that's God's angel!" I protested sub-vocally.

He's male. Don't listen. Then she let go and swam away from me.

Don't listen? Don't listen to what? To the wrathful angel? It wasn't his words I feared, but his sword. However, I signaled the others to hold back.

Sylvie swam close to the angel. He raised his sword threateningly. "That applies to you too, infernal nymph." Then he paused, listening. I heard the faintest trace of a devastatingly familiar song. The siren was singing to him! Faintly, so as not to catch the three of us, but definitely singing. Could this possibly work?

I clapped my flippers to my ears to block off the sound, and Sinbad and Duban copied my motion. They understood the siren's eerie power.

The angel sheathed his sword and ran after her. Then he spread his arms in a swimming motion and lifted off the ground. It looked as if he were flying. As he was, in effect.

Sylvie continued her song as she swam just out of his reach. I saw that she had reverted her tail to legs, flashing him as she had us. That was less efficient for swimming, but considerably more efficient for luring. And, compelled by the eerie, potent song, he was going for it. He was indeed male, and it seemed no male could resist the siren's compelling call. He had probably been on solitary duty for millennia, and really missed the pleasures of female company.

I shook myself out of my reverie. "Forward!" I tried to shout, but only blew off my breathing mask. Water rushed in, and I choked and coughed before I got it back in place. But Sinbad and Duban got my message, knowing that Sylvie had cleared the way for us. Allah might not be pleased at such time as he found out, but maybe he would understand that we were on a vital mission.

We swam on toward the island, I mean hill. Soon we reached it, and closed in on the tree. It was a widely spreading, handsome thing, with lovely, thick foliage.

Then a giant serpent appeared, slithering out of a hole in the ground. "Begone, sons of Adam!" he shouted. "Before I chomp you to death!"

A serpent speaking in human language? But he certainly looked big enough to do the job. We paused again.

Then I remembered how a serpent had spoken to Eve, and tempted her with the forbidden fruit. This must be part of that serpent's punishment: to guard the tree forever, in case someone bypassed the water and the angel with the flaming sword. Allah evidently did not believe in half measures.

"Ah, I see you are surprised I speak your language," the serpent said. "But I was educated in your country, in Bagdad."

Bagdad? Not Baghdad? He was faking it, and had made a foolish error. But he was still big enough to eat us all.

I will handle him, Nylon thought. Then she slid off my finger, formed into a truly voluptuous lady serpent, and slithered by the male serpent with a come-hither wriggle that even I found evocative. Something about the way she disported her curves.

Mesmerized, the serpent followed her. What else could he do? She was emulating his ideal mate. This was her area of expertise, and there was none to match her in this respect.

We swam on to the tree and checked through the foliage. It had only one fruit on it, of an unfamiliar type, but it looked absolutely delicious. Yet I knew we couldn't eat it; we needed it for the ship. I swam up and plucked it with my flippers, and put it in my backpack with the spare air. Then we swam hastily away, uncertain just how long Nylon could distract the serpent.

The return was routine. We simply swam to the surface and waved to the ship. The Flying Dutchman sailed to us, and in moments we were hauled back on deck. Soon Sylvie and Nylon reappeared, having completed their diversions, and I wrapped them around my fingers. Best of all, the swim had washed off the stink of the cursed perfume and we were approachable again.

Next question: how did we feed this fruit to the ship, since it didn't eat? It was amazing how such an obvious challenge had never occurred to us beforehand.

"Feed the figurehead," Jewel suggested.

Maybe that was it. The figurehead was the bust of a merman with a noble brow and piercing gaze, surely a Dutchman, whatever that was.

We squeezed the fruit and caught the juice in a cup. Then I held on to the prow of the ship, swung around before the figurehead, and put the cup to the Dutchman's mouth. I tipped it. Much of it spilled down off his chin, but some soaked into the cracks around the mouth. Then the mouth opened, and more went in. The figurehead was animating!

"Well done, King Aladdin!" the head said. "Now get out of my face."

I was so surprised I almost fell into the sea. I scrambled back to the deck. How had this wooden thing not only come to life, but known my name?

The figure turned his head around and gazed at all of us. "What's this I see arrayed before me? Several idiotic oafs and some fair maidens, so at least it's not a total loss."

"Now wait a minute!" I protested stupidly. "We're not idiots!"

The figure focused on me. "Oh yes you are," he said with infinite scorn. "And fools to boot. You wasted your entire effort."

That began to get to me. "How can you say that? You're just an old wooden carving. What do you know?"

"I know everything," he replied. "Because I have just tasted of the forbidden fruit of the Tree of Knowledge."

"The tree of—?" I began, stunned.

"Yes, you utter dope! You sought the Tree of Life, but you got the wrong tree! You were too dull to get the hint when you encountered the Serpent associated with it. Instead of recharging your ship, you bequeathed the knowledge of the universe to its figurehead. You are simply too stupid to live."

I exchanged a glance of sheer dismay with the others. I was indeed an idiot.

CHAPTER SEVEN

Jewel came to my rescue. "Knowledge or not, Aladdin is still the master of this ship, and you must do his bidding."

The figurehead, once a wooden statue but now animated supernaturally, laughed. He tried to throw back his head, but was limited in his range. He settled for a curt nod. "Foolish woman. I know everything, including the nature of the curse that binds this ship and those who serve upon it." It now closed its eyes and mumbled something incomprehensible. "There. The curse has been properly reversed. I am my own captain and I have freed those who were forced to serve on board."

Indeed, before our very eyes, the many ghostly sailors that populated the ship began disappearing.

"Then how will you steer your ship without a crew?" demanded Sinbad, stepping forward.

"Fool! I *am* the ship."

And with that, the main sails sprang open. I saw the ship's wheel turn rapidly on its own volition, and the great ship began moving with the wind.

"And thanks to your foolish king, I have been revivified, too. As they say, two birds with one stone."

"Where are you taking us?" I asked, as the ship began picking up speed, cutting across the wide lake.

"Here is a riddle for you, King Aladdin: if one possesses all of the knowledge of the universe, what is left to learn?"

I blinked, stumped, aware that, in my haste to procure the sacred fruit, I might have inadvertently doomed the entire earth. As the hot desert air blasted over me, as the distant shore sped rapidly past, I could think of no answer other than, "Nothing is left to learn."

"Precisely."

"But that does not answer my question: where are you taking us?"

"He's taking us to the one being who can still teach us something," said Duban, stepping forward.

I blinked at the lad, always surprised to hear the deep wisdom that came from his innocent face.

"He is right, of course. From the mouths of babes and all that," said the figurehead, grinning. "The earth no longer holds much interest for me. And certainly there is nothing left to gain from humans." He suddenly raised his once-wooden arms, and as he did so the ship lifted from the lake and took to the air.

"But I don't understand," I said. "What being? Where are we going?"

And then it hit me as we rapidly rose into the sky, higher than we ever had before.

"Allah," I said.

"Allah, God, the Creator, the Source, whatever you want to call him, for he goes by many names," said the figurehead, shouting above the wind. "We're going to Him, and I know just where he resides."

———

We moved away from the figurehead and gathered near the bow as the ship continued steering itself. Booms swung and sails trimmed. All on their own accord. Somehow, I found this more frightening than when the ghosts had performed the same duties. Below, the hot desert sand quickly fell away. Now whole mountain ranges came into view. We were higher than we had ever been before, and only going higher. The air up here seemed far more difficult to breathe. Indeed, I saw Sinbad taking deep, futile breaths.

Queen Nylon and Sylvie Siren both sprang from my fingers, transformed in mid-air, and landed deftly on bare feet.

"The air is indeed thinner up here, Aladdin," said Queen Nylon, responding to my thoughts. "Soon, none of us will be able to breathe. Although Sylvie and I are immortal, we cannot survive long without the elements of earth. In this case, what is known as oxygen."

"Where is it taking us?" said Jewel. Her neck was beginning to strain with the effort of breathing.

"I read its mind," said Myrrh. "A scary mind. Full of wild notions. But one notion stood out above the others. He's taking us to a hole in the sky. He calls it a wormhole. He believes it will take us to another dimension, as he calls the place where Allah resides."

"We are familiar with such portals," said Sylvie Siren. "And I assure you, that humans aboard a flying ship will not survive. In fact, it is doubtful that Queen Nylon, Nydea and I will survive."

The air was getting noticeably colder—and stronger. And even as the wind thundered over us, it seemed deprived of this crucial oxygen, of which Queen Nylon spoke. Apparently, this element was necessary for thinking straight, because my brain seemed even more stubborn than normal.

But one thought did surface and I turned to my son immediately. "Duban, can you fashion more breathing devices?"

The boy nodded and tried—but apparently his magic also needed this precious oxygen. My mind raced, and seemed only to be growing foggier and foggier. Wind and clothing billowed as we all began shivering. Below, the mountain range looked like nothing more than a crack in the dirt. The desert itself was just great swatches of yellows and browns. On the far horizon, I could see the great sea appearing.

How much time did we have before all the oxygen in the air was gone, or before we all froze to death? I didn't know, but

I gathered it would be soon. My brain seemed to be shutting down.

"I have a suggestion," said my blessed wife suddenly.

"Hurry!" I gasped.

"The ship claims to have all knowledge of the universe…" she paused, gasping for air. "And now seeks the presence of Allah, the source of all knowledge."

"Go on," I urged.

"Then let's tell him a story," she said, and I could see the cords standing out on her neck as she struggled for air. "A story in which he does not know the ending."

"I don't understand—"

"Yes!" shouted Myrrh, catching on immediately. "He might be all-knowing but he cannot possibly know how our story would end."

"And to hear the ending, he must abandon his journey to Allah," said Duban.

Perhaps I was the dullest and thickest of them all, but it surely seemed like all had caught on to the idea faster than I. But when my wife's wisdom finally blossomed in my oxygen-deprived brain, I saw the beauty of it.

"A story without end!" I shouted. "But who among us is the greatest storyteller?"

"I will do it," said Jewel. "I've been telling Duban stories since the day he was born."

With that settled we all appeared at the ship's figurehead, who turned and looked at us scornfully. "Enjoy your precious few minutes alive, humans and nymphs. One way or another, you will meet your maker." It faced forward again and closed it eyes.

"Perhaps," I said.

"There is no *perhaps*," said the figurehead, this time not even bothering to turn toward me. "You have nothing that I want, and there's nothing that you know, that I don't know."

"Except one thing," I said.

Now I had its attention. It turned toward me and seemed amused. "And what is that, King Aladdin?"

"The conclusion to our story."

"I know all stories," it said dismissively.

"But not *this* story," said Jewel, stepping forward.

CHAPTER EIGHT

I wondered what kind of story Jewel would tell. She was a woman of many qualities, but I had not heard her do this before. I hoped it would not be some soft, dull femalish narrative.

"Once upon a time, there was a sweet girl named Idris," she began.

Oh, Hades! But we were stuck with it. All we could do was listen, and hope the arrogant figurehead found it interesting. Because otherwise we were all doomed.

———

Idris Ifrit was one of the djinn kind, of which there were many in the old days. She was a carefree creature, floating about the landscape, a playful adventurous spirit with more than a hint of mischief. Since she could assume any likeness she chose, she was outstandingly pretty when in human form. She especially liked to tease mortal men by pretending to be one of their kind until they tried to hold her and kiss her; then she dissipated in smoke and laughter, leaving them aroused without satisfaction. What a joke on them!

One day she happened upon a mortal king as he went his way, traveling from one city to another with his retinue. She had heard of him; he was Solomon, reputed to be very wise. She could not resist testing that; was he smart enough to handle an alert air spirit? She assumed solid form, bypassed his guards, entered his tent, and flashed him with her outstanding young body.

"And who are you, fair maiden?" he inquired, interested. Mortal men of any age were interested; it was their nature, just as it was her nature to tease them.

"I am Idris," she said, letting her garment slide down to reveal an increasing amount of her ripe torso. "Idris Ifrit."

He did not seem surprised. "So you are one of the djinn kind."

"What of it?" she asked, dropping her garment to her waist. In a moment he would be under her spell, as any mortal man would be.

"You are banned from my kingdom."

"Really?" She let it drop the rest of the way. "And what are you going to do about it?" She took a breath that was likely to make his mortal eyes pop out. She so loved teasing pompous men!

"This," he said, catching her arm with his hand. Then, before she could dissipate into smoke, he crammed her into a tiny green bottle. She had not known he could do that; no other mortal could. By the time she turned around inside it, he had put in the stopper and sealed it with his royal seal. She was unable to push out; the seal was powerful magic. She was caught.

This was a lesson she would not soon forget. This king had the power to enforce his edicts. "All right," she said. "I will leave your kingdom. Now let me out."

But she discovered to her horror that he was not even paying attention to her. He simply tossed the bottle into a bin with hundreds of other bottles and went to sleep. No amount of hammering against the green glass sufficed; he didn't care.

The bottles contained other djinni, male and female, no more able to escape than she was. She could see them struggling with growing despair. What a monster this Solomon was! He certainly had no sense of humor about a little innocent teasing.

In a few days the bin of bottles was unceremoniously carried in a wagon to a ship in the harbor. The ship took the collection out to sea. There, far from land, it was dumped into the choppy waters. The bottles were all made of heavy glass; they slowly sank.

Some were swallowed by fish; some disappeared into the gloom below. Hers was caught by a wayward current and borne swiftly away from any possible land.

She was helpless. She prayed to Allah, the glorious, the beneficent, the compassionate creator of the three worlds to free her, but there was no response. All she could do was settle down for a long nap. Until, somehow, Allah grant that she be released.

Between sleeps she pondered, and it occurred to her that she had been somewhat irresponsible in her treatment of mortal men, and perhaps deserved a rebuke. She resolved to mend her ways, and to treat all people, even mortals, as fairly and kindly as she could. That did not win her a release, but she held on to that resolution, for it seemed apt.

She had no notion of how much time had passed when her bottle washed up on a distant foreign beach, but suspected it was many centuries. She was of course immortal; time hardly mattered, except that she was bored. She peered out through the glass, hoping for the best.

And there came walking along the beach a Daughter of Eve, a living girl, maybe thirteen mortal years of age. Hope flared; would she see the bottle? Would she pick it up? Would she break the seal and uncork it?

The girl paused. Idris signaled wildly inside the bottle, trying to catch her attention. And it worked! The girl spied the bottle and picked it up. She peered into the glass and saw Idris. She smiled.

That was awkward, because now Idris saw that though the girl's body was typical of her kind and age, on the verge of nubile, her face was not. It was misformed, with the features present but in the wrong proportions. In fact she was ugly.

Then the girl applied her teeth to the cork and pulled it and the seal off the bottle. Idris poured out, puffing into smoke, then forming into her natural shape. Oh, it was good to stretch, after all this time confined!

But business before pleasure. There was a protocol. "Young miss, I thank you for releasing me," she said. Of course she spoke

in the girl's tongue, because ifrits could do that without even trying. "I am Idris Ifrit, cruelly imprisoned by King Solomon long
ago. In return for the favor you have done me, I must do you a
similarly significant favor. What do you ask of me?"

Surprisingly, the girl did not demand a mountain of gold or
the man of her dreams or a kingdom to rule. All she said was: "I
am Idrin. I'd like a doll."

"Idrin? That's close to my name!" Idris realized then that
there could have been a magic tow, drawing her bottle close to
one who almost matched her name, so that it was not coinci-
dence. But that hardly mattered. "A doll? You're too old for a
doll."

Idrin sighed. "I will never attract a nice man, or any man.
I'm too ugly. So I might as well remain a child forever. I'd like to
have a doll as pretty as you. Then I could love her forever."

Idris opened her mouth to protest again, but realized that
the girl was being realistic. Mortal men were notoriously fickle;
about the only thing they valued more than a pretty face was a
pretty bosom or bottom. Still, a doll?

"I'll see what I can do," Idris said at last.

"Don't steal it!" Idrin said quickly. "I'm not a thief."

"I will find it or make it myself," Idris agreed. Then she dissipated and searched the area for a lost doll. But there turned out
to be nothing suitable; the only thrown-away dolls were broken
or malformed. She returned empty-handed.

"I have not found a doll," she said. "So I will make you one."
She shrank into a doll-sized image of herself. "Will this do?"

"But that's you!" Idrin said. "I didn't mean to imprison you
again. You need to be free."

Idris had never cared much about any mortal person, but
there was something about this girl that appealed to her. "I can
stay this way until we find a real doll for you. I was in the bottle
hundreds of years; I can be a doll for a few days."

"Oh thank you!" Idrin exclaimed. She picked up the doll and
hugged and kissed her.

Idris found that she liked that attention. The girl's feeling encompassed her. Mortals had more intense emotions than immortals. Idris was satisfied to remain near her, bathing in that joy.

Idrin walked toward her home, carrying the doll, singing a little song of joy. It was amazing how little it took to make her happy.

Then a boy crossed her path. "Oh, that's Bull," Idrin muttered. "He's trouble."

That was another accurate assessment. "Hey, foulface!" Bull called. "What you got there? I bet you stole it."

"Did not," Idrin responded, trying to avoid him.

"Yeah? Give it here!" he snatched it out of her grasp.

"Don't hurt him!" Idrin said. That set Idris back. She had been about to stun the bully with an electric eel charge.

Bull laughed coarsely, misunderstanding. "This here's a girl doll, not a boy doll, and I'll hurt her if I want." He put a hand on each of the doll's arms and made as if to pull her apart.

Oh? Idris got ready to turn into flame and scorch his hands.

"No!" Idrin cried. She was just too much of a pacifist!

"Yes!" Bull retorted, again misunderstanding. He wanted to torture Idrin before actually dismembering the doll, not knowing that was impossible.

Idris thought fast. How could she stop this implacable bully without hurting him? Then she got a notion. She was in direct physical contact with him, so this was easy magic. She reversed his emotional polarity.

Bull paused, taking a moment to reassess. He had never experienced anything like this before.

Then he returned the doll to Idrin. "I'm sorry; I was only teasing. I would never hurt your doll." He took a breath. "Or you."

Idris stared at him, confused. The bully was making nice? But Idris clarified it for her. "I reversed him," she whispered. "I made him want to help you instead of hurt you."

"Idrin," Bull said. "Please—may I kiss you?"

Now both girl and ifrit paused in shock. Idris was the first to figure it out. "I'm rusty. I have been too long out of practice. I overdid it. I put him into love with you."

"But no one loves me," Idrin murmured.

"Please," Bull said. "I'm not good at this. I want to hold you and kiss you. Please let me." Such was the power of the magic, he was asking instead of taking. He wanted her return interest.

Girl and doll gazed at him. What were they to do? It would be chancy to change him again; magic seldom reversed cleanly, especially when wielded by a rusty practitioner. But Idris knew, if Idrin did not, that Bull was about to ask for more than a hold or kiss.

They were in trouble.

———

Jewel paused in her narration. The ship had drifted lower as the figurehead listened, providing them all better air to breathe. The story was working. I was amazed that such a soft, gentle tale would interest the knowledgeable figurehead, whose heart, let's face it, was wooden. It seemed that Jewel knew what she was doing after all.

But would it be enough to prevent the figurehead from resuming his quest for Allah? I did not know, and feared to ask.

CHAPTER NINE

"Why did you stop?" asked the figurehead, turning its massive head to regard Jewel.

The entity, which had once been a carved wooden statue projecting from the prow of the ship, now appeared to be a combination of living and inanimate. Its face was still lined with wood grains, but now it was very much alive, and expressive enough to show his arrogance and now his irritation.

What manner of being he was, I didn't know, but just as the thought crossed my mind, Sylvie's words appeared: *He is the Flying Dutchman's original captain, sire. Forever cursed to remain on his ship. Indeed, cursed to forever inhabit the ship.*

An unbreakable curse, I thought. *Which is why he was unable to free himself.*

Yes, sire. Only the gods can save him now.

There's something else, Myrrh thought. *That figurehead knows but is not telling you: only you, as master of the ship, can free him from the ship, by officially granting him release. He knows you won't, so hides that information. He has nullified much of the curse, but must remain with the ship, regardless where he takes it. Unless he can indirectly kill you and plead to Allah for release.*

That was interesting. I still had some power. I was about to ask why he had been so cursed when Jewel spoke. Her weariness did not feel feigned, although I suspected it might have been. "I stopped because I have grown tired."

"Nonsense."

"I'm short of breath, as you can see. We are much too high for me to continue the story."

"Never mind that, then, woman. We shall proceed."

And with that, the ship veritably lurched forward, surging through the heavens, toward this reported wormhole that I suspected would be our doom. I leaped forward, struggling for my own breath, for we were indeed very, very high. No doubt this valuable oxygen was quite low up here.

"But wait," I said. "You do not know the ending to the story."

"It is just a story. A fair one, mind you, but a made-up tale nonetheless. Unimportant in the grand scheme of things. Indeed, it is time to meet Allah."

And the ship surged forward.

I cudgeled my oxygen-deprived brain and continued with the logic I had started, "Unimportant or not, it is something you do not know. It is knowledge that's unknown."

"What are you getting at, mortal?"

"You would be approaching Allah under false pretenses. You claim to know all, but you don't. You don't know the ending to Jewel's story."

"I can guess the ending. I am aware of all stories now, thanks to your epic blunder. Most stories are not so different."

"Guessing is not the same as knowing," said Myrrh, stepping in. "You ate from the Tree of Knowledge. Not the Tree of Guessing."

The one-time captain looked from Myrrh to me, then threw back his head as far as it would go. "Damnation!"

Our forward momentum stopped so suddenly that many of us were thrown into railing or into each other. Once we had regained our balance, I saw that the great vessel was now adrift in the heavens. Below, the earth was nothing more than splotches of color. Browns and tans where the earth lay, blue where the ocean rested. White patches of clouds drifted everywhere. All of us were gasping for breath. Little Duban was looking green. We needed to reverse course immediately.

"What do you propose, mortal?" growled the figurehead.

"Jewel will finish the story as she sees fit," I replied. "After all, such stories cannot be rushed."

"You are toying with me, mortal."

"We are striking a bargain. You get your story and we get what we need."

"Your lives."

"More than that," I said. "We get the services of your magnificent ship."

"And if I refuse?"

Jewel stepped forward, leaning heavily on me. "You will never know the ending to Idrin's tale."

"Damnation and ruin! Fine, mortal, you have yourself a deal. And when, pray tell, will I hear the next installment of the story?"

"Tomorrow night," said Jewel. "When I have properly rested."

The wooden figurehead swore, then threw his head to the right, and the ship turned to starboard, and soon we were speeding rapidly down through the heavens. Below, the earth quickly took on more and more details, and as we plunged down through the clouds, we all took a deep and blessed breath.

"Where to now?" growled the figurehead, when the ship had leveled out many hundreds of feet above the desert sands.

"The Hinterlands," I said.

Now the figurehead grinned mischievously. "To stop those who seek to unlock the Gates of Hades, I suppose."

"Yes, of course." It suddenly occurred to me that if the ex-captain had knowledge of all things, then he certainly knew where the key was.

His disdainful laugh seemed to support my line of thinking. "And do you not realize that the Key to Hades is actually—"

And in that moment, Dea the Slave, who had been standing nearby, rushed forward and pointed across the bow. "Dragons!"

Whatever the figurehead was about to say had been lost, for the moment. He snapped his head around, as did I. Sure enough, swooping from high above were three black dragons, each more hideous than the next, and all sporting massive, leathery wings and long necks.

Sensing what was about to come, I used my sash to strap myself to the nearest railing and ordered the others to do the same. What happened next was a testament to the ship's construction, although I suspected it was now held together by magical means. At any rate, the ship veered away from the dragons so sharply, that I thought my neck might snap. The aerial maneuvers that followed were enough for all of us to heave whatever was left in our stomachs. And when we were not heaving, I watched in amazement as the great ship, easily two or three times the size of the dragons, always just managed to avoid the black beasts.

When one dragon lunged, belching a great stream of crackling fire, the ship would turn sharply to starboard or port, or dive and plunge. Each time the fire would just miss us, always leaving a burning black trail in the sky where we had once been.

Our bodies twisted and turned and strained against belts and sashes and rope—anything that we had found to secure us in place. At one point, the ship plunged deftly, just as two of the magical creatures slammed full board into each other. I turned my head and watched as they spun wildly from the sky.

From where had the creatures come, and why? Only once had I seen such foul beasts in the land of man, and they had been the work of powerful djinns. Such creatures, I knew were commonplace in Djinnland. So why were they here now? Who had summoned them?

The final dragon screeched in fury and beat its powerful wings and soon closed in on the starboard side. The side I just happened to be on. I had a good look at the beast's pure black eye, an eye that revealed nothing. Its snout was as long as three horses and its nostrils impossibly wide. From them, black steam issued forth, and I suspected I knew what that meant.

As it had just turned its head, I could see the smoldering fire from within ignite. By Allah, it was going to torch me alive! I think the figurehead realized that, too, and perhaps realized he might never hear the end of the story, for just as the beast threw back its head to let loose with a great blast, something else blasted.

Cannon fire.

The ship rocked with the percussion, and so did the dragon. Its great black eyes bulged, and the fire winked out. It massive wings went limp, and now I could see the great, bloody hole in its side.

It fell from the sky, quite dead.

The Flying Dutchman leveled out and I saw that the figurehead looked eminently pleased with himself.

I unfastened myself from the railing and checked on the others. They were fine, but bruised. Duban had a bloody bump on his head, where he had knocked it against a mast.

I headed straight for the figurehead.

"You know who sent the dragons," I said.

"Of course," it said smugly. "I know everything. Just as I know where the key presently is."

"Tell me," I said eagerly. "Who sent the dragons? Where's the key?"

Now the figurehead threw back its head, just narrowly missing the wooden hull. "And where would the fun in that be, King Aladdin? You are not the only one who can play games."

And with that the figurehead faced forward again, and the ship turned slightly to port, racing over the shifting desert sands and into the setting sun.

CHAPTER TEN

Jewel retired for the evening and night, for she really was tired, unsurprisingly. I joined her, of course. "Do you have a good continuation of the story?" I asked.

"Why would I tell you, with the ship listening?" she retorted. "The story must remain untold, until I tell it to Captain Figurehead."

Good point. "In that case—"

"What part of 'I am worn out' do you not understand?" she demanded sharply. "Besides, there's the baby."

She was on to me. I sighed. This was going to be a long nine months.

"Oh, don't be like that," she said. "Find a concubine. That's what they're for."

That was an idea. "Maybe that new girl, Dea," I suggested.

"Don't touch her! She's dangerous."

"But you know I can't be potent with just any woman who isn't you. She has to be special."

"That is your problem," she said unsympathetically. Women can be like that. "Now let me sleep."

Ahem, Queen Nylon coughed mentally.

I had for the moment forgotten that she was on concubine duty. She would certainly do. "Good night, Jewel," I said, and left her presence. Fortunately we had a spare cabin.

Nylon unwrapped herself from my finger and assumed the form of Jewel. She kissed me. "Let me show you what I would do with you if I weren't with child," she murmured.

She showed me, because of course she was not with child. It was quite a night. The only way I would have known she wasn't Jewel was that she lacked the cutting verbal edges Jewel evinced when annoyed. Nothing I did annoyed Nylon; she seemed genuinely delighted to accommodate anything I could imagine. There is something to be said for interacting with a woman with centuries of experience and a hunger for renewed passion.

Next day the ship was back over the desert and flying west. It did not seem to be moving as rapidly as before. "Is there a problem?" I asked Captain Figurehead.

"I'm tired, dolt," he said. "I need a story to refresh me."

So he was dawdling, to make sure we did not arrive at the Hinterland before the story was finished. If we wanted to arrive there in time to prevent the Key from being used, we would have to get on with the narrative.

Fortunately Jewel was now up for it. Maybe she had literally dreamed up the continuation during the night. She settled herself in a deck chair near the figurehead and began talking. The rest of us joined her there, hoping for the best.

"It has reached me, O auspicious Captain," she said formally, "that when Idris Ifrit invoked a spell to reverse the bully's emotional polarity, she got it slightly off-center and instead of merely feeling helpful, he had fallen in love with Idrin. This was awkward…"

Idris snapped her fingers, freezing the bully in place, unaware that he was being paused for their convenience. It was minor magic, but useful in a situation like this.

"Oh, what am I to do?" Idrin whispered to Idris. "I can't kiss him. I don't even like him. Besides, I'm too young for that sort of thing."

Idris knew that in many locales girls were considered marriageable at ten years of age, and Idrin was three years beyond that. But it was her duty, as part of her return favor for being released from the bottle, to see that the girl was satisfied with the outcome. So if romance was not what she wanted at this time, so be it. The bully had to be turned off.

But how? Messing again with his emotional settings was not advisable, lest it lead to even more difficult complications. Yet what else was there? Idrin didn't want him hurt, and that blocked off whole avenues of actions.

Then she remembered a standard ploy utilized by attractive women to stave off suitors without actually rejecting them. "Tell him that if he wants to kiss you, he must perform three heroic feats in your honor, like single-handidly defeating an army using no more than the jawbone of an ass, or taming a rogue dragon."

"That's cheating," Idrin objected. "I have to play fair. There should be only one demand, a relevant one, and it should be feasible to accomplish with reasonable dispatch."

Idris took a breath and counted to twelve, so she wouldn't explode into a roiling cloud of acrid smoke. This child was frustratingly fair-minded. In fact she would be an excellent partner for any man, regardless of her appearance. But that was the rub: men did not care much about excellence of character, only appearance. Men could be such dolts that it was remarkable that any woman ever chose one to marry. Except that the Sons of Adam in some locales had gotten around that by depriving woman of all rights, so that they were not in a position to choose.

And therein lay the clue. Give the bully a task that contributed to Idrin's appearance, making her beautiful. Then she would be able to choose any man she wanted, when the time came. And if the bully did not accomplish that task, then he got no kiss. Win-win, either way.

"Demand a pot of beauty cream," Idris told the girl. "The magical kind that makes any girl's face lovely."

"Does such a thing exist?" Idrin asked skeptically.

"Yes, because I am about to make some. I will hide it under a stump. If he finds it, you will use it and it will make your face beautiful. The rest of your body will fill out nicely in the next year or so, so you will need no more than the facial."

"But suppose he doesn't find it?"

"Then you don't have to kiss him."

"But what if he finds it?"

Idris counted mentally to thirteen. "Then you will have to kiss him. You can do that much. If he wants more, he will have to perform another task, one more challenging. By the time he accomplishes that, who knows—you might even begin to like him a little."

"Never!" Idrin said with dismaying certainty. But she seemed taken by the idea of challenges. "I'll do it."

Idris snapped her fingers, reanimating the bully as she converted herself to a jar of cream and hid under a nearby stump.

"Please," the bully said. "Anything for a kiss."

"Anything?" Idrin asked.

"Anything."

"Then fetch me a jar of beauty cream. Then you may have one kiss."

"But I have no idea where such a thing would be," he protested.

"There's one in this vicinity. Maybe you can find it."

"Stay right here," he said. "I will find it."

Idrin would have preferred to go home, but she waited. It was just barely possible that she was intrigued by the idea of becoming beautiful, and possibly even by the prospect of submitting to a kiss. One never could be certain of the content of a girl's mind or heart.

The bully looked diligently, propelled by his desire for the kiss. He turned out to be a fairly efficient searcher. He crisscrossed the area, checking every clump of weeds and around every tree, shaking the foliage. And in due course he kicked over the old stump and found it. "Haa!" he exclaimed as if he had found something as precious as gold, and actually, he had.

He brought the jar back to Idrin. "Here it is. Now my kiss."

"Not yet," she said. "I must make certain it's the real product." She opened the jar, dipped out some cream, and smeared it on her face. Then she brought out her pocket mirror and looked.

The smear of cream crossed from her left eyebrow to her right ear. Most of her face was ugly, as before, but where the smear was, her face was lovely. The cream really was magic, as Idris had formed it from her own magical substance.

The bully stared, amazed.

Idrin quickly smeared the cream across the rest of her face, and in that moment she became beautiful, as her mirror verified. The cream had filled out the cavities and smoothed out the lumps and left matchless skin covering perfectly formed features.

Well, he had delivered. Idrin knew she was stuck for it. "Now you may kiss me," she said, nerving herself for the ordeal. She had never kissed a boy before.

The bully gazed at her. Then he shook his head. "Those are no longer the features I love. I don't want the kiss any more." And he turned about and walked away.

Idrin stared after him, relieved but also, if truth be told, just a bit annoyed. She had been rejected *because* of her beauty?

Idris Ifrit re-formed as the doll. "My spell made him love you exactly as you were at that moment," she explained. "He still loves that face, but you no longer have it. If you want him back, you will have to wipe off the cream quickly before it sets."

But the girl hesitated. "Let's not be hasty," she said. She realized that if she left the cream on, and it set, she would be lovely for the rest of her life. She would be able to attract any man she wanted. That counted for something.

So she walked on to her home village, carrying the doll. Soon another boy spied her. He was handsome, one she liked. "Who are you, fair miss?" he inquired.

"He does not recognize you, because of the change," Idris murmured.

"I am—visiting my friend Idrin," Idrin said.

"Let me show you the way," the boy said. "In exchange for a kiss."

Oops. Idrin liked the attention, but she remained too young for what she suspected a kiss would lead to, and wanted to take it slowly. So she temporized. "Maybe after you do me a significant service."

"And what is that?" the boy asked eagerly.

"Uh—" She stalled.

Idris had to rescue her. "Make him fetch you a wonderful ship upon which you can travel the world in luxury and leisure."

Flustered, Idrin repeated the request almost verbatim. Had she had time to think about it, she would have pared it down closer to a rowboat.

"Immediately," the boy said. "But where can I find such a ship?"

Idrin listened to Idris' whisper. "Well, Noah's Ark might be nice. I understand it still sits stranded in the Mountain of Ararat, not far north of Baghdad. It might need a few repairs, but it is the world's premium ship."

"Immediately," the boy agreed, and set off forthwith. Little did he know what he was undertaking. Boys were like that.

"I think I won't be needing the doll after all," Idrin said. "You have given me more than enough, Idris, and I thank you."

"In that case, I'll go help the boy with the Ark," Idris said, regretting that she had sent him on what might be an impossible mission. "That should prove to be an interesting quest, regardless of the outcome."

"Thus concludes the tale of Idris and Idrin," Jewel said. "Idrin was destined to grow up, marry, and live happily the rest of her life. But the tale of the boy's quest for the lost Ark is even more wonderful, filled with rare adventure, foul tragedy, and fair maidens. But I am tired, and must rest until the morrow."

"This is a cheat!" Captain Figurehead said angrily. "You are starting another tale without giving me a chance to digest the first one."

"And you don't know the outcome. What a pity," Jewel said without pity. "Carry on, Captain."

I saw that she had the figurehead snared. She would keep telling tales until we got where we were going and did what we were doing.

Now all we had to do was get to the Hinterland in time to accomplish our mission, assuming that we'd be able to do it despite the somewhat surly cooperation of the figurehead. I feared the boy of the tale would have an easier time finding and renovating the Ark.

CHAPTER ELEVEN

As the days passed, as we headed deeper and deeper into an empty wasteland filled with endless rolling sand dunes, Jewel regaled the ship and crew with her tale of the boy's epic search for Noah's Ark.

I marveled again at my wife's cleverness. After all, a search for one great ship as told to another ship of equal greatness was sheer genius, although I questioned the wisdom of her need to constantly remind the accursed captain that Noah's Ark was, indeed, the greatest of all ships. But my wife spared no fools, least of all me. The ship, although knowledgeable of all things, seemed predisposed to surliness and haughtiness, proving again that great knowledge did not equate to great wisdom.

Lucky for us, Captain Figurehead seemed enraptured by the tale of the boy and his search for Noah's Ark, and so for now we continued sailing over desert dunes, the occasional oasis, and the even rarer caravan.

On this evening of the third day of our journey, as we ate cheeses and breads and fruits and nuts, Jewel cut short the latest installment of her tale, this time leaving the boy stranded in a catacomb of tunnels deep within Mount Ararat. The captain was clearly frustrated. Even I felt mildly annoyed at having to wait another day to hear of the boy's fate. I sensed we were reaching the end of the captain's patience. What would happen after that, I didn't know. But it might be a battle of wills.

Others on board listened to the story; in particular, Dea the slave girl, who seemed particularly enchanted by the tale.

Now, as the sun began to set, Duban brought out his lyre and struck up a somber tune. Although he was now the heir to my throne, I doubted that he would take the job. He was more minstrel than monarch, despite being one of the more powerful conjurers of magic I had ever seen.

He is the last of his kind, said Queen Nylon in my ear, no doubt following the trail of my thoughts.

"What do you mean?" I asked, sub-vocalizing my words.

The prophecy, my lord. Your stepson was prophesied to be the last of the great magicians, following a long line of great magicians. With him, the bloodline will die. It is why Prince Zeyn was so determined to hurry the process up.

"You make it seem like he won't see his next birthday," I said, perhaps a little louder than I had intended. Jewel shot me a curious look, raising her eyebrows, but I did not elaborate. Already Jewel was getting used to me speaking seemingly random gibberish to my nymph counsel.

Queen Nylon, however, had grown curiously silent, and I did not feel the need to press the matter. Instead, I watched the boy play on happily, tapping his foot, smiling at the others who had joined him. I had grown found of him, and the thought of him dying prematurely was a devastating one. I could only hope Queen Nylon was wrong.

———

I had been dozing lightly on deck as Duban played on, when I felt a small tug on my sleeve. It was Jewel. "Look," she said, pointing. "It appears the slave has made a new friend."

I followed her pointing finger and, although it was now late evening, could easily make out the form of Dea speaking urgently to the Captain Figurehead. The captain tilted its massive head toward her, clearly listening.

I sat up, curiously alarmed. "How long have they been talking?"

"I don't know. I only just noticed them."

What business did a slave girl have with speaking to the accursed captain? I didn't know, but I called Duban and Myrrh over. He quit playing and they came over together. I spoke telepathically to Myrrh to shield my thoughts, asking her to relay them to Duban, which she did.

Can you fashion a listening device? I asked my son.

Duban nodded once the message had been relayed. *Of course, father.*

I explained further what I needed, and he nodded again and slipped his lyre inside his robe where it promptly disappeared. He next held both hands over his ears and closed his eyes. Jewel gasped first, followed by me. After all, a hairy, wolf-shaped ear now appeared where the boy's once roundish ear had been. The wolf-ear perked up and promptly pointed toward the figurehead and slave girl.

Duban listened a moment, then reported: *They're striking a deal, father.*

What kind of deal?

He listened some more. *It's an exchange of some sort. His services for...*he trailed off, listening again. *His services for freedom from the curse.*

That surprised me. I had been expecting to hear something else. "Sylvie," I said, sub-vocalizing the word.

Yes, sire?

"I thought you said only a god could reverse his curse."

Indeed. His was one of the most powerful, placed upon him by yet another god. You were given power over the ship, by one with equivalent power, so if you did it you would be acting on a god's authority.

"Then how could a simple slave girl free him of it?"

A good question, sire. Perhaps she's more than a simple slave girl.

I thought about that as Dea nodded toward the figurehead, and slipped back into the shadows.

———

Curiously, the next evening, after spending the whole day speeding along at a much faster clip, the accursed ship captain did not request Jewel's presence to continue the story. Clearly, the captain had abandoned his desire to see Allah. His deal with Dea had something to do with that.

Jewel and Myrrh came to my side, where I stood with Sinbad at the ship's helm. Jewel was sweating profusely and holding her stomach.

"What's wrong?" I asked, coming to her.

"She needs rest, sire," said Myrrh, looking at my wife with obvious concern. "I'm worried for her."

"It's nothing, really—" but her words were cut short with a gasp of pain.

Surely, a journey to the Gates of Hades was no trip for a pregnant woman—or any person with an ounce of sanity. Now, as my wife did her best to push through the pain, I came to a decision. I rounded up the remaining passengers—all those who had so willingly volunteered to help. I explained to them that I could no longer risk their lives and, despite their protests, ordered them to board the smaller dhows.

Once all were aboard, I kissed my wife and rubbed her growing belly—luckily, her pain was subsiding. Duban hugged Myrrh tightly, and Sinbad held Nydea. Shortly, the smaller boats peeled away and shot down through the sky. We would remain in contact through Nydea, who was always magically connected to Queen Nylon. A good thing, since we would have had no other way of finding them.

Now the three of us watched as the two dhows, filled with the remaining crew, raced downward until they finally disappeared from view.

Now it was just myself, Sinbad, Duban and the two nymphs on my hand. A motley crew, but a battle-tested one. Whatever the hell was going on here, we would find out. And whoever sought to open the Gates of Hades, we would stop.

One way or another.

Sinbad suddenly pointed across the bow. "The Hinterlands, Aladdin."

I turned my head and saw them, too. Great, rocky crags jutting up from the desert floor, rising high into the sky. Buzzards circled above, wings outstretched. The ship seemingly picked up speed.

"And what of the Gates of Hades?" I asked.

"It is rumored to be deep within a cave, beyond a fiendish underground river."

The River Styx, my lord, said Queen Nylon. *Or the river of hate. It separates the world of the living from the world of the dead and is guarded by the dog-beast, Cerberus.*

"And ferried by Charon," I sub-vocalized. "Yes, I know my Greek mythology."

Sinbad turned to me. "Things are about to get very interesting."

CHAPTER TWELVE

We sailed slowly beside the mountain range, looking for caves. The curvature of the Hinterland terrain was intricate and bleak, with many false avenues. Beyond it was nothing but trackless burning desert. "I wonder how anyone gets here," Sinbad said, "without a flying ship?"

"I suspect most of them are dead," I said. "So they can navigate the desert without suffering ills of the flesh."

"Or they are magically drawn in by Hades and don't need to look," Duban said. "We are approaching by an alternate route that should be rarely used."

Good point; there were not too many flying ships in these parts. If all dead folk had to go to Hades, why would it be made difficult for them to find? It was living folk like us it wanted to discourage.

"There," the figurehead said, nosing the prow toward the forbidding recess of a dark cave that resembled nothing so much as a cavity in one of the tooth-like mountains.

We looked. He was surely correct. We would have to verify it.

That brought something else to my mind. What about the Flying Dutchman? Could we afford to leave the ship while we explored the cave? I did not trust that, but did not want to discuss it aloud with the figurehead listening. He had behaved okay recently, but that might be a pose to get us to depart peacefully. I did not trust him. The ship was bound to me, but Figurehead *was* the ship and might be able to override the binding and go his own way. If I were not there to tell him no. Magical strictures can be devious.

Sinbad seemed to read my thought. "Let's draw lots for the privilege of rear-guard duty," he suggested. "In case something unkind is on our trail."

Instead of lots, we cast dice, which were more convenient. High throw would stay on the ship. Sinbad won it, and no, I'm pretty sure the dice weren't loaded. Not to put too fine a point on it, but I am familiar with loaded dice. I wasn't certain whether Sinbad was disappointed or relieved to be left behind, but concluded that he felt more at home on the ship. Besides, I thought Duban and I were the best team to handle this particular chore, partly because I carried the ringed nymphs.

Yes, we make you halfway competent, Nylon agreed.

No man is sufficient without the guidance of a woman, Sylvie added.

That was not precisely the way I would have put it, but I decided not to argue the case. They were probably teasing me anyway.

And you like being teased by pretty women, Nylon thought smugly. She had me there, though the type of teasing I preferred related to "accidental" exposure of private parts rather than disparagement of my nature.

We'll keep that in mind, Sylvie thought. As if she hadn't been well aware of it all along.

"I'll circle around and keep an eye on the area," Sinbad said.

Duban and I took a dhow and glided down to the cave. The *Dutchman* moved on, but we knew it would return when needed.

It was a black hole. I was nervous about entering it blind, but Duban came to my rescue by snapping his fingers. Then a glow appeared, emanating from the walls and floor, making the path clear enough for us to proceed.

The back of the cave narrowed into a passage just about big enough for me to walk comfortably. It twisted on into the mountain, until the light of the entrance was no longer visible. So far, so good.

Then I heard a weird howl. It sounded like a trio of sick wolves. "What's in there?" I asked nervously.

"Cerberus," Duban said succinctly.

Now I remembered: the dog with three heads. "Um, I wonder," I said. "Do we really have to face that?"

"We do if we want to reach Hades."

"Do we actually have to reach Hades? There's nothing in there that we want. What we want is to see that the Thief of Baghdad, or whoever else has the Key, doesn't get there. We can intercept him out here."

"Maybe, father," Duban agreed. "But suppose there is more than one access to the Gates?"

He's got a point, Nylon thought.

Smart lad, Sylvie agreed. *I'll be his mistress some day.*

"Oh, fudge," I said, borrowing one of Jewel's expressions. "There could be a dozen routes. We can't guard them all. We'll have to guard the Gates themselves."

"That was my thought," Duban said.

"Which means we have to deal with that dog."

"I can stun him, and you can cut off the heads one by one."

I had another thought. "If I do, won't that alert the proprietors of Hades that something is amiss? They might not take kindly to someone mistreating their guard dog. I prefer this mission to be quiet."

I can do it, Nylon thought. She unwrapped from my finger and dropped to the floor. "I will need to see Cerberus, and for him to see me," she said.

I had confidence in her ability. We moved on toward the sound. Soon we came to the cavern where the monster canine lurked. He was the size of a pony, and each head was uglier than the others, with sharper canines and more lather. The noise of their howling was horrendous, this close. The smell was worse.

Cerberus spied us and charged, all three heads slavering hungrily as sparks flaked off their gnashing teeth. I couldn't help quailing. Fight this monster? Without Duban's stasis spell

I'd be lucky to lop off one head before the others chomped me to mush.

Nylon formed into a three-headed female dog. She howled in her bitchiest harmony. Since her nature was to perfectly emulate any male's fondest desire, she got Cerberus' attention immediately. He changed course to orient on her. But she immediately moved into a side passage, one head looking back coyly. He followed eagerly. She was a pro, all right. But I couldn't help wondering whether she led me on similarly, and for similar reason: to distract me from whatever else I might have on my limited mind.

Of course she does, Sylvie reassured me. *Men have to be managed, for their own good.*

I let that pass. What else could I do?

We were alone. We moved on.

We came to the River Styx. It was a dark thread of water coursing through the cavern, broad and sinister. There was a musky odor to it, not unpleasant.

"Charon must be around somewhere," Duban said. "I think the river entirely circles Hades, or at least the entrance to it. Charon could be anywhere in that loop."

"Do we really need Charon?" I asked. "I don't see why he would ferry us across, considering we're not dead. Maybe we'd be better off swimming across it on our own."

"Don't do that!" a voice called.

We turned. There was a cloaked figure approaching us from the tunnel we had just left. Then she threw the cloak open. It was the slave-girl Dea! "What are you doing here?" I demanded. "I sent you away for your own safety."

"I appreciate that," she said breathlessly. Oh what an effect her violent breathing had on her low decolletage! "But I had to warn you. Something I remembered, belatedly, too late to tell you."

I was still on a prior track. "How did you get here?"

"I took a dhow. We had an extra. Now about that memory…"

"How did you even know where we were?"

"Your dhow was parked outside. But this thing I remembered—"

"Remembered?"

"About the River Styx. It's poisonous, and the River Lethe is a tributary. So if you try to swim in it, if you don't die of poison, you will slowly forget why you came here, and then who you are. Souls that try to escape run afoul of the water and lose their identities and drift around helplessly. That's why there are no escapes from Hades."

"No escapes," I echoed thoughtfully.

"And even the fumes of its surface will have a similar effect, only slower. That's why Cerberus stays clear. I was afraid you would try something stupid, like swimming or rafting across it, and be doomed. So I came to warn you."

Smart girl, Sylvie thought.

And I had been about to do exactly that. Her warning was well taken. "But Charon is not likely to ferry us across," I said. "I suspect he has a thing against living folk."

"He does," she agreed. Her breathing had slowed to normal, but somehow the curvature of her forward architecture was more visible than ever. I remained considerably intrigued. "But Charon also has magic to nullify the fumes so that the ferry passengers don't lose their minds as well as their lives. You need his help to cross."

Ouch. "Let me consider," I said. Then I asked Sylvie, mentally: *Does this make sense to you?*

Actually, it does, she agreed. *But I don't trust her. That frontal exposure is no accident. She's flashing you. She may just have wanted to get you alone, so made up a pretext. That's a female device.*

A female device. The siren should know. I didn't trust Dea either; there were surely holes in her story. On the other hand, she was one superlatively winsome creature, and I needed practice getting potent with concubines who weren't the image of Jewel. If Dea was as intrigued by me as I was by her...

Don't touch her, Sylvie warned. *I'll tell Jewel.*

So now the siren was the guardian of my morals.

Well, its a dirty job, but someone has to do it.

I sighed. *I'll keep my hands off her,* I thought. *This is not the ideal place, anyway.*

Besides which, Nylon may return at any moment and catch you.

That, too. Nylon had become just as proprietary as Jewel. I had to return to legitimate business.

"So what does your siren doxy say?" Dea asked knowingly.

Doxy? Sylvie raged. *I've got half a mind to reassemble and tear out some of her hair.*

"Don't do that!" I said.

"Oh? Just let her try it," Dea said, evidently making a shrewd guess. "She'd be a fish out of water."

Oh, is that so? Well—

Was I about to have a nasty cat-fight on my hands? "Please, ladies! This is no place to argue. We need to figure out the best course."

"Exactly," Dea agreed, adjusting her shirt to be less confining.

We can't cross anyway without Nylon, Sylvie reminded me.

Dea glanced at my hands. "Where's your fairy queen slut?"

WHAT?! Sylvie thought, outraged by the affront to her friend.

I had to get things back on track. "What do you recommend?" I asked Dea.

CHAPTER THIRTEEN

The River Styx, although black as night and hidden deep within the mountain, glowed softly. I saw why: glowing spirits circled the river, flying or walking or even sitting on the many boulders that clustered near the river's bank.

They were not given proper burials, said Sylvie, *and must now roam the river's bank for one hundred years.*

I shuddered at the thought of roaming this bleak landscape for so long, when Dea spoke: "My lord, we need to gain access to Charon's ship, of course."

"'We?'" I said. "You're not going anywhere. This is far too dangerous for you."

Dea turned on me, bristling. "But you are willing to risk bringing a boy to the Gates of Hades?"

I considered the absurdity of the situation. At any other time, a slave girl would have bowed before me without daring to look up until commanded to do so. Now, one was questioning me. Such talk would have landed her in a dungeon—or, with a less forgiving king, the loss of her tongue or even her life.

You are a long way from your palace, Aladdin, said Sylvie. *Although I do think the slave girl does need to be reminded of her place.*

I sighed. Rank and stature had no place when one was standing on the banks of the River Styx, with a three-headed beast running free in the tunnels, and the Gates of Hades nearby. Instead, I put aside my ego and said, "Duban has special…skills. He is of use to me."

"As do I, my lord," said Dea, and all challenge left her, to be replaced by something far more…seductive. She took a deep breath and her chest lifted and fell and somehow her lips seemed to grow even fuller. My mouth went dry.

She's a pro, said Sylvie.

She's beautiful.

Oh, brother.

As three distinct howls reverberated from one of the tunnels, Dea turned suddenly and marched off toward the river, where, to my surprise, a man appeared out of the gloom. He was guiding a simple wooden ferry, poling it with practiced, efficient strokes. Charon had a long, gray beard and a bent back, and white skin that seemed to glow. He was obviously a very old man.

Not a man, my lord, said Sylvie. *He is a lesser god. A demigod, to be exact. The son of Nyx and Erebus.*

Duly noted, I thought, and realized I was seeing my first god. I'd certainly seen my share of djinns and nymphs, but never a god. Other than pushing the ferry along with obvious grace and skill, he looked no different than any other aged man.

Except he's been ferrying the dead for eons, Sylvie reminded me.

God or not, that didn't stop Dea from boldly approaching the river's edge. Charon, who had been leaning heavily on the pole, snapped his head around when he caught sight of Dea approaching. He quit pushing the ferry along and now he drifted in the center of the gently-flowing river. As he drifted closer, I could see that he was not alone. Three or four souls were huddled together on one end.

Dea boldly waved him over. In the process, she somehow managed to look both intoxicating and vulnerable. She was also showing a lot of flesh, and I wondered just how often Charon saw live women. Judging by the proliferation of spirits along the river—and the few souls on his ferry—I didn't think very many times. Perhaps the lesser god did have a weakness for living flesh. If so, the luscious Dea would surely push him over the edge.

Oh, brother, said Sylvie, clearly picking up on my thoughts.

"She's a threat to you," I sub-vocalized, "and therefore you don't like her."

I don't trust her, said Sylvie. She paused, then added, *And I don't like her.*

I chuckled lightly, despite the seriousness of the situation, and now watched in stunned amazement as Charon guided the ferry away from the center of the black river and toward her along the bank.

She's doing it, I thought.

Men are all the same, thought Sylvie. *Gods and mortals alike.*

I chuckled again as the ferry pulled up along the bank. Water lapped over rocks…and hissed. Truly accursed waters. There was a short exchange. Dea giggled. A soft, whispery voice responded, and to my shock, the ferryman to the Underworld actually smiled. A moment later, Dea rejoined our group.

"He will ferry us," she said.

"For what in return?" I asked.

Dea slipped next to me and nearly laid a hand on my chest. Instead, she stood on tip-toes and whispered into my ear: "You just let me worry about that, sire."

No doubt she struck a sordid deal, my lord, said Sylvie contemptuously.

I swallowed and nodded, and suddenly found myself envious of the ancient ferryman. I could only imagine the pleasures that awaited him. It was the way she had whispered into my ear. Her hot breath. It had sent a shiver coursing through me that did not readily abate.

Get hold of yourself, sire. We've got serious business to attend to.

"Yes, of course," I whispered. "But what about Queen Nylon?"

The queen can take care of herself, sire. Cerberus is not the first beast to be smitten by her charms. If I know the nymph queen, she's got that puppy wrapped around her finger, panting somewhere.

And for the third time, I chuckled as we followed Dea to the ferry, and boarded along with her under the watchful eye of Charon. Shortly, he pushed off and soon we were adrift on a mostly calm river. Huddled near the prow of the ferry were three souls, two of which I immediately recognized. They had, after all, been ghostly sailors aboard the Flying Dutchman. Now released from the curse, they were heading to their rightful place in the Underworld.

Duban kept close to me. For all his talents, he was still a little boy—and a frightened one at that. I rested a hand on his head and he moved closer to me still.

A cold breeze moved over us. Glowing spirits were seemingly everywhere, lighting the way eerily. Charon methodically poled us forward, occasionally stealing glances at Dea. We appeared to be approaching a dark tunnel. I shuddered to imagine what lay beyond the tunnel.

Sylvie's words appeared in my thoughts. *Sire, do you see anything different about the slave girl?*

Her name is Dea.

Either way, do you notice something different?

Dea stood apart from us, staring forward, seemingly lost in her own thoughts. She gripped her hands behind her back, playing with various rings on her fingers.

What about her? I asked.

Her rings, sire.

What about her rings?

Sylvie sighed heavily. *Are men oblivious to everything?*

"Out with it, nymph," I growled under my voice. "What about her rings?"

They were not there before, sire.

"You're certain?"

I'm certain.

The rings were thick and golden and looked remarkably similar to the ring presently on my finger, the ring that was, of course, Sylvie.

"Magical rings?" I asked, sub-vocalizing the words.

Undoubtedly, sire. Of course, there's one way to know for certain.

"How?"

Touch her. I can learn a lot by touching someone. Just as I know all of your deep, dark secrets, my lord.

As we neared the black tunnel—a tunnel where the waiting spirits appeared not to venture—I stepped over to the slave girl and lifted a hand to rest on the girl's shoulder.

Not that hand, Sylvie chastised, sounding remarkably like Jewel. *Your other hand. The one with me on it.*

"Oh, right."

I lifted my other hand and placed it on Dea's shoulder. The slave girl flinched and spun around. When she saw me, her almond-shaped eyes widened with pleasure.

"Hello, my king. To what do I owe this pleasure?"

As I was about to open my mouth, Sylvie gasped in my mind. So much so, that I was immediately disoriented. I gave Dea a faltering smile.

"I wanted to thank you for your help," I said, stumbling slightly over the words.

"Anything for you, sire," said Dea, bowing her head slightly.

I smiled again and backed away, just as the ferry plunged into the dark tunnel. A light flared from nearby, and I saw that Duban was holding a magical ball of light before him. Allah bless the boy.

"Now," I said to Sylvie, just under my breath. "What was that all about? What did you learn?"

She is no slave girl, my lord.

"Oh, who is she?"

You have just met your second god. She is Medea, the goddess of desire and lust, and the two rings on her finger are none other than The Thief of Baghdad and Sinbad. Both, I suspect, are now under her complete control.

"Control how?"

Sex slaves, sire. Perhaps for all eternity. And if my guess is right, she desires you next.

Sinbad! But what could have happened? I didn't know, but I wondered if my friend had been ambushed on the ship.

And one other thing, sire, thought Sylvie. *She wears the Key to Hades around her neck.*

CHAPTER FOURTEEN

I knew I was in trouble.

If the Sorceress Medea had made a deal with the Dutchman Figurehead, and seduced and ringed both the Thief of Baghdad and Sinbad, she was bound to be too much for me. I remembered her from mythology, the wife of Jason of the Golden Fleece. When he deserted her, she butchered their children. She was a completely cynical and ruthless creature, now bent on further mischief. No wonder she had seemed unalarmed about the kraken; she must have summoned it to harass the sirens while the Thief of Baghdad stole the Key to Hades. As I saw it, I had only one advantage, if you could call it that: she did not know I knew about her.

And you have me, Sylvie thought. *We sirens do have powers, though not in the same league as the sorceress.*

"Powers?" I sub-vocalized.

We can swim well, she reminded me. *We can enchant men. And I can shore you up against being seduced by her.*

"Even if I think she's the sexiest creature on two legs?" Because I did. "Even if I really would like to be seduced by her?" Because I would. "Even though I know better?" Because when did knowledge that it was dangerous ever stop a man from desiring a beautiful woman?

Yes. I can run interference to prevent her from seducing you by force, as she must have done with Sinbad. I can sing the anti-summons song, the reverse of our normal lure, to make you averse to such seduction. But there is one thing I can't do.

I knew there would be a catch. There always was. "What is that?"

I can't stop you from sending me away, if that's what you decide to do. I occupy your finger by your sufferance. You have to want me here, or at least tolerate me.

"I do want you here! How could you think otherwise?"

Aladdin, she thought seriously. *If she persuades you to send me away, I will have to go. Then I will not be able to protect you. I must not leave your finger, even for an instant, because then she will strike and you will be lost.*

I appreciated the warning, uncomplimentary as it was to my defensive ability, which echoed my own concern. Medea was more than any mere mortal man could handle alone. "I will not let her persuade me," I promised.

I sincerely hope that is the case, for both of our sakes. I dare not swim in the River Styx.

"Neither dare I," I agreed.

One more caution.

"Another?" I asked, dismayed. "Isn't our situation bad enough already? I know I must not do what I would so dearly like to do."

Indeed. But you have to appreciate that seduction is more than sexual.

"It is?" I asked, surprised.

It is. You think it's like making out with a harem girl, for physical gratification without any larger commitment. But the more dangerous form is emotional. You can be lost without having any sexual connection. Don't let her seduce you emotionally. Don't fall in love with her.

"Love!" I echoed, appalled.

Dea—that is, Medea—turned to face me. "Love?" she inquired. "Did I hear you correctly, sire?"

Oops. In my excitement I had forgotten the sub in subvocalize and spoken aloud. "I doubt it," I said. "I suffered an uncomfortable belch I was unable to suppress." Not that there was anything wrong with a good belch after a meal. It was the nether belch, the breaking of wind, that was such a serious social

blunder that men had been known to flee the region, humili-
ated, after letting one slip out audibly in public. A proper belch
was a compliment to the server of a good meal. But it was all I
could come up with at the moment.

"It certainly sounded like love," she said smoothly, taking my
hand.

Sylvie shot out what felt like a jag of lightning. Dea withdrew
her hand, shocked. Literally. She did not seem pleased.

"No, it was more like gas," I said, embarrassed. I had not
known the siren could do that.

"If you have indigestion, I'm sure I can help," Dea said, ooz-
ing concern. "I have a potion."

Don't take that potion!

I was not about to. "Thank you, but I'm sure it will clear," I
said. Then, to Sylvie I subvocalized "I will take Duban's hand.
When we have contact, you update him on what we have
discovered."

I will.

Duban was of course standing beside me. I took his hand.

"Isn't that sweet," Dea said with mixed sympathy and irony.
"He comforts his son."

Dea had not been with us long. With luck she would not
realize just how powerful a magician Duban was. That could be
another secret weapon. Once he knew the score.

Done. He says thank you for the secret weapon compliment.

Oops. She must have relayed my ongoing thoughts along
with the background. At least now Duban had been updated. I
hoped he could match the sorceress, forewarned. But I feared
what her seductive powers could do to him, inexperienced as he
was in this respect. Medea was doubly dangerous.

"I hope the siren slut doesn't shock him, too," Dea murmured.

I'll let that pass, Sylvie thought. *She's trying to make me get so mad
I'll unwind from your finger and tackle her physically. She would then
make short work of me—I'm no sorceress or goddess—and then make
shorter work of you.*

76

Surely so. "Stay with me," I told Sylvie. "And if you remain in touch with your home base, you should inform them of our situation."

I will, she agreed. *But sirens are sea creatures; this region is inaccessible to them. They have to be carried, as I am with you.*

Then I had another thought. "The women!" I subvocalized. "Jewel, Myrrh, Nydea. What has happened to them?"

Bad news, Sylvie agreed. *They would not have simply let the sorceress take over. She must have done something with them.*

The three were by no means helpless. Nydea was a Nubile Nymph like Nylon, Myrrh was telepathic, and Jewel was very much her own woman at all times. But they had not known they were up against a sorceress. I had to find out. Would Dea tell me? Well, maybe I could use some subtle male persuasion. "How's my wife doing?" I asked her.

"She is—resting," Dea said. "As are the others."

"Resting? Surely not the whole time." Then, to cover my knowledge of Medea's identity and nature, I added "I prefer to think that my wife is unable to relax during my absence."

She smiled beguilingly, her eyes infinitely more appealing than almonds, and her lustrous hair seemed to ripple like a flowing river. "Surely she dreams of you, you handsome hunk. What woman wouldn't?"

Yuck! Sylvie thought, using an expression new to me, but I caught her meaning. Dea was laying it on too thickly, figuring me for the dolt I often am.

Still, the architecture of her upper torso, now so close under my nose, was compelling. As long as she was playing the role of a sex slave girl, maybe it would be safe to—

Stop it!

I sighed again. Sylvie was right, of course, unfortunately.

"We can't do much while under the watchful eye of the ferryman," Dea murmured. "But a kiss or two shouldn't hurt, if you can muzzle that bitch of a fishtailed ring for a while. It would be a shame to waste slack time." She inhaled, and I swear her luscious mounds increased one or two sizes. "In fact, we could dance." She turned into me, and my hand fell naturally to her marvelously slick silk-covered posterior. My hand couldn't help it; such an artifact was designed to be appreciatively stroked. She moved against me, and I felt an evocatively warm caress wherever her alluring body touched mine.

This time the zap was so strong there was a crackle as sparks jumped. I did not feel it, but it was evident that Dea did. I almost thought I saw tiny curls of smoke rising from her breasts and bottom.

"But I think you will have to remove the ring for the time being," Dea said, not showing her discomfort. "Just put it in your pocket if you don't care to drop it in the river."

Don't do it!

"I can't do that," I said, with not entirely faked regret. "I promised to take care of the siren while she is in my charge."

Dea shrugged as if the matter were of little moment, though I knew she was seething. She was a consummate actress. "Then perhaps another way." She lifted on her lovely toes and kissed me.

I was amazed by several things. One was the compelling power of the contact; it was as though a piece of heaven was touching my mouth. Another was the response the siren made. I heard a truly eerie song, and felt the current of a lightning bolt passing between our lips, magnetizing them. Sylvie was shocking Dea, and this time the sorceress was fighting back with her own current. The battlefield was my mouth. I felt as if my very skull was glowing, radiating light.

Medea was trying to seduce me by force, right there standing on the raft on the River Styx, and Sylvie was fighting it. I was almost a spectator. But I felt the rising compulsion of passion. I was being drawn into hopeless love with the sorceress. I tried to resist, but it was like opposing an elephant with a single finger. It was plain that I was vastly over-matched, as Sinbad must have been. This creature had centuries of experience taming rebellious men.

For eternal moments the combat continued. The sorceress was strong, very strong. But the siren had the home field, as it were, and my cooperation; I was on her side, for what little that was worth. It was an impasse.

Then Dea broke the kiss. "Or maybe not yet," she said. "But soon, I think."

She's not fooling, Sylvie thought, and it felt as if she were gasping. *I can't take much more of that. She's too strong.*

So the contest had been defined. Medea intended to seduce and conquer me, and had the power to do exactly that, and Sylvie could not stand against her indefinitely. I needed to think of some other way to protect myself, or we'd all be lost.

Now the raft was emerging from the tunnel and coming to the inner shore. I was pretty sure that the closer we got to the Gates of Hades, the weaker our position would be. We needed to do something to turn the tide. But what?

CHAPTER FIFTEEN

I am Queen Nylon, ruler of the Nubile Nymphs in Djinnland, and bound to King Aladdin of Agrabah. Although I am ruler in another realm, I do not wish to see destruction befall earth. After all, many of my nymph sisters—including the mischievous Sirens—live in this physical plane. Not to mention I desire to one day live life as a mortal.

To this end, I will stop at nothing to save the earth from those who seek to destroy it or subjugate it with unspeakable horrors and evils. I may not be as powerful as the gods or goddesses, as the sorcerers and sorceresses, but I do possess *some* skills.

And I will use them freely and willingly.

Now, after leading the great three-headed beast away from the others and deeper into the labyrinth of tunnels, I suddenly came to a dead end. The tunnel was narrow—just wide enough for me to turn and face the beast as it wildly rounded the corner.

As is often the case for me, I had assumed the form of the female desired by a nearby male. I don't transform automatically. Meaning, the transformation is always a choice—and I've spent the greater part of my life embodying some very interesting females. Admittedly, a three-headed bitch was one of the more interesting incarnations.

Cerberus filled the narrow tunnel, each head hunched low and dripping foam. Muscles rippled along his powerful shoulders and flanks, muscles that I immediately felt a strong attraction for. As is always the case, whenever I embody another woman or creature—if I allow the embodiment—I always feel a powerful sexual attraction to the male desiring me. Now was no different. Three heads suddenly seemed like a brilliant idea—the better to admire my mate. The powerful, sleek, muscular body, with claws big enough to disembowel an elephant—looked majestic, and exciting.

Cerberus came closer still. His three heads swayed a little, sniffing the air. Foam dripped from his three muzzles. Never had I seen a more powerful creature in all my life. And I found it so very exciting.

He paused before me and one of his three heads tilted to one side as its ears perked up. The other two heads watched me closely, still growling just under its breath. Its center head was doing the thinking, while the other two remained on guard. Indeed, I closely associated with my own center head. The other two seemed almost independent, although I was aware of everything they were seeing and sensing. A strange sensation, at best.

But I wasn't putting much thought into the strangeness of having three heads. In fact, I wasn't putting much thought into anything at the moment. I was focused on the creature before me. The powerfully perfect canine approaching me, whose deep-throated growls filled the small space.

He came closer still, his body tense, ready to pounce. I knew my magic was such that I was his ideal female, his greatest love, if possible. Would that be enough to spare my life? I didn't know, and so I waited.

His claws clicked on the dust-covered floor. His growling turned into chuffing and snorting. And then the center head dipped forward and his thick ears folded back.

And Cerberus, the great guardian to the Underworld, nuzzled me affectionately.

———

The nuzzling didn't last long.

Cerberus reared back, growling deeply from his three throats. Words next appeared in my mind, which did not surprise me. Many of the magical and supernatural entities who inhabit the earth and Djinnland alike speak telepathically.

You are a nymph.

Indeed I am, Great Cerberus.

You lured me from my post.

I did.

Why?

Admittedly, I was having trouble focusing. I was fully invested in this incarnation, and the powerful site of Cerberus was making thinking and speaking difficult.

There are those who seek to unlock the Gates of Hades, I thought. *We are here to stop them.*

Fool! It is my job to stop them. No one gets past me unless I leave my post. And thanks to you, I have.

Heady thoughts of amour quickly dissipated from my thoughts. So much so, that I returned to my regular form. *What do you mean?*

The head to my left closed its eyes and the beast grew silent. *They are crossing now. I can see them now. Damnation.*

Yes, I quickly thought. *My friends are indeed crossing. To guard the gate—*

One of you is very much not a friend. One of you is not who she claims to be. One of you is a god. You have been used and manipulated, and I was just foolish enough to fall for your shapely tail. The three heads growled deeply.

I did not know—

Of course not, nymph. Mortals and even immortals should never play in the realms of the gods. Now, climb on my back and let's go.

I did as I was told, and soon we were racing back through the tunnels, twisting and winding, and I was suddenly thankful to be riding high upon the great guardian, for I was certain I might have been endlessly lost.

Cerberus picked up on my thoughts. *A good thing for you, too, since the Minotaur that roams these tunnels is not nearly as forgiving as myself.*

Soon, we were back in the massive cavern, where we could just make out the form of a ferry laden with both human and non-human passengers. Cerberus raced along the river bank, following the ferry, but already it was moving further and further out, heading directly toward a dark tunnel in the cavern wall. The river sounds swallowed the great beast's thunderous barks.

Cerberus next sent out a powerful telepathic message that blasted through my own skull, but the old man continued to pole the ferry steadily, ignoring the three-headed guardian.

Damnation. He's been enchanted.

I dismounted, frustrated. *By who—*

And then I saw her. Dea was standing near the others, looking forward, hands clutched behind her back. She seemed to be playing with a ring.

Cerberus read my thoughts. *Except her name isn't Dea. She's Medea, goddess of lust and temptation. And those aren't rings. Those are mortals, whom she has enchanted.*

Can we swim to them?

The water is cursed and will quickly drive us insane. My master, Hades, does not appreciate the living entering the realm of the dead. Master will not be pleased. I have failed him.

We watched from the river's bank as the ferry moved further out onto the black water, growing smaller and smaller. A cool wind swept over us, except it wasn't really a wind. It was the many souls waiting impatiently for their time to cross into the Underworld.

Not all was lost. Not with Aladdin and Sinbad around. Yes, Aladdin played the part of the simpleton wonderfully. In truth, he was a surprisingly resourceful hero, one whose exploits would be sung and written about for years to come. Sinbad was no slouch either, and they had Duban, too. They were a formidable trio.

Perhaps, thought Cerberus. *Except the boy is no match for a goddess and Sinbad has fallen under the spell of Medea.*

Damnation indeed! I suddenly thought of the magical dhow, and just as the image of the flying lifeboat came to me, one of Cerberus's thick heads began nodding.

Interesting, he thought. *We can't swim across the water, but we could fly across.*

There were dhows on the Flying Dutchman, but I had no clue where the ship might have anchored, or even if Captain Figurehead would give me permission to board, which I doubted.

Perhaps the dhows that had transported the women and passengers were still available. They had not returned, which was not surprising. After all, if we never returned for the others, Jewel and company could use the magical vessels to escape the desert, perhaps hopping from one oasis to the next.

With the river surging nearby, I cast my thoughts out to my sister nymph, Nydea, but got no response. I tried again and again but got nothing.

Cerberus, who was the offspring of gods himself, turned to me. Or, rather, his center head turned to me. *I sense a sleeping spell, nymph. But they are not far. I suggest you climb on and we go to them. At once.*

I did, and soon we were plunging back through the tunnels— and out into the bright sunshine and the heat of the desert sun.

CHAPTER SIXTEEN

I blinked in the glaring light, getting my vision back. I saw that Cerberus was doing the same; all three heads were facing away from the sun and squinting their eyes. Soon all four of our heads cleared and we were able to look around the landscape.

The dhows were gone, both the one we had used and the one Medea must have used; they had naturally returned to their father ship when no longer occupied. We had only to go to the *Flying Dutchman* to get one of those life craft.

On my way, Cerberus agreed, and started running. He knew where the ship was because of his telepathy.

Or did he? There should be no one aboard the *Dutchman* now; the girls had been sent away by dhow for their safety, and the rest of us had then entered the cave. But I didn't question the big dog's direction; that would soon clarify one way or another.

We rounded a foothill and the ship came into sight, floating about treetop height above the level sand of the desert. Cerberus ran toward it.

"Wait!" I protested belatedly. "That's the ship. We want the women." I realized that Captain Figurehead was unlikely to give us a dhow to go to the women; Medea would have told him no.

They are there, the big dog responded. *Verify it yourself.*

I checked mentally for my sister nymph Nydea. She remained asleep, but there was no doubt: she was aboard the ship. How could that be?

I worked it out: Medea had been with Jewel, Myrrh, and Nydea. She must have enchanted them with her sleep spell, then piloted the dhow to the Dutchman. The figurehead would have taken them aboard, having made a deal with the sorceress. Then she had enchanted unsuspecting Sinbad, putting him on her finger beside the Thief. Nothing like keeping your captives close.

There had remained only Aladdin, Duban, and the other two nymphs: Sylvie Siren and me. Medea had evidently nullified some of them, too, or was in the process. I had escaped mainly by accident. But at least now I could rescue the three sleepers.

We came to a stop immediately below the ship, and I dismounted. "Ahoy!" I called. "Descend so we can board."

Captain Figurehead peered down at us. "I don't answer to you, slut," he called back. "Or to any three-faced cur. Begone." The ship remained well out of reach, bobbing gently on some invisible tide.

Just so. "I was afraid of that," I murmured to Cerberus. "He answers to Aladdin, or maybe now to Medea."

And your allies are asleep, the dog agreed. *I had not anticipated this pass.*

"None of us did," I said. "But we need to find a way, or the Gates of Hades will be unlocked and opened, and that will not be good for the world." That was a considerable understatement. I tried not to show my desperation, but of course he knew it.

I know something of your kind, Cerberus thought. *You assume the aspect of any male's fondest desire, as you did with me.*

"A three-headed bitch," I agreed. "I regret that I could not be your mate in reality. I did not mean to disappoint you."

You have not disappointed me. You are *granting me my fondest desire.*

"Not at the moment," I said ruefully.

Yes, at the moment. I want a bitch of my own kind, yes. But I am also centuries lonely for responsive companionship. You are the first to talk to me as a person, to treat me as an equal without being terrified or repulsed.

86

"You *are* a person, and an equal," I said, surprised. "You surely know that."

I do know that. But nobody else does. Except you.

Now I saw it. Cerberus was a figure of fear and horror, deliberately, so as to be able to be the most effective of guardians. But that was indeed a lonely mission. I needed his help, yes, but I also had a fundamental respect for his nature. As he understood by reading my mind.

Yes.

"And if you could become a mortal dog and live an ordinary mortal life guarding some minor prince's property, you would gladly retire to that," I said. "Just as I would retire to being a mortal concubine, giving up my position as the immortal Queen of the Nubile Nymphs. Immortality gets dull after a few centuries."

Yes.

"So we do understand each other." I took a breath. "I am glad to have encountered you, Cerberus. But now we have to find a way to board that ship."

I was getting to that, before we drifted. You can be all things to all males.

"I can, to a fair extent," I agreed. "But they have to be within reach."

Including an animated figurehead?

I paused in place, physically and figuratively. The figurehead was not really a living thing, but he had been given a magic elixir that had brought him partly to life. He had once been a living captain. Could I charm him?

He must be lonely too. There are very few animated figureheads, and I doubt they get to commune together often.

"Excellent point," I agreed. "I'll try it. He will know what I'm doing, because he knows almost everything, but males are foolish that way. He may not be able to resist."

Males are foolish, Cerberus agreed.

I walked out so as to stand in front of the ship, facing the figurehead. "Captain!" I called.

"Oh, don't try your wiles on me," the figurehead said impatiently. "I know what you are, trollop."

"Indeed you do, Captain," I said, assuming the form of a female figurehead mounted on the prow of a lady ship. "But don't you get just a bit jealous to see all my attention wasted on other males, ignoring you? When you know more than all the rest of them combined? Is it fair that you be ignored merely because you are cursed to be forever glued to your ship?"

"It's not fair, harlot," he said bitterly. "Now stop trying to play me. I know what you are up to."

"Of course you do, Captain," I agreed. "But you also know that you are unlikely ever to get another chance to be kissed by any fair female of any type. Certainly not Medea, who you know will use you and discard you. Only a nymph of my kind will actually deliver. So come down and let us board, and I will give you a kiss to remember forever. This is paid love, but isn't it worth it?"

"Damn you, whore!" he swore. "I shouldn't even listen to you!"

I spread my arms wide and pursed my lips. I kissed the air. "You curse me with foul epithets because you resent that I am not giving my love to you. But you can have a token share of it, for a price. Paid love delivers," I repeated.

Furious with himself for being tempted, he drifted lower. He was male, and this was his fatal weakness.

True, Cerberus thought. *It is what gives females their power.*

I kissed the air again. Figurehead came down another notch, as if drawn on a line. I inhaled, and his descent accelerated. All the knowledge in the world did not matter in the face of his foolish desire. "What I offer is at least honest," I said persuasively. "A fair exchange, both of us understanding its nature."

Finally he landed. Cerberus quietly circled behind, ready to board the ship. Meanwhile I stepped into the figurehead, embraced him, pressed my luscious body against his carved one, and kissed him with an ardor he knew was false but that still transported him. Ever thus, with man and woman. The irony was that because his body was still mostly wood, he could not actually *do* anything with me beyond the kiss. All he could do was dream.

"You're such a manly figure," I murmured, supporting his pretense. It was a lie, and he knew it was a lie, but he couldn't help appreciating it. Men and women both live for such lies.

"I would give up everything else, just to have this be real," he said.

"Of course you would," I agreed, stroking his hair. "Look at it this way: you are real to the extent that you are male. A non-male would not care about my touch. Maybe Medea will lift your curse and enable you to be mortal again."

"Maybe," he agreed longingly.

"Now please allow me to board your vessel."

Now he was canny. "Why should I do that? I already have your kiss."

"You know the answer to that, Captain. It is because when we leave your ship, I will kiss you again, in appreciation."

"I do know that," he agreed. "It's a cheat, but I can't help it."

"True." I disengaged, then walked to the side, caught hold of a rope ladder dangling there, and climbed up to the deck.

Cerberus was there, having bounded up with one powerful leap. *They are locked in their cabins.*

"Then we shall release them, in more than one sense," I said.

The cabins could be barred from inside or outside. I removed the outer bar to Jewel's cabin and entered. There she was, on her bunk, sleeping like the enchanted queen she was. "Jewel," I said.

There was no response. Darn! I needed a magical key to unlock the magical spell. Then I remembered the traditional way to break such a spell. I leaned down and kissed her on the lips.

Nothing happened. Darn again; that garment was torn.

Then I remembered: it normally required a *male* king or prince to perform the kiss. I was royal, but of the wrong gender.

Then I got a notion. "Cerberus," I said. "Do you have any royal lineage?"

Of course I do, he agreed. *Somewhere a millennium or so back there was a royal hound who just couldn't resist my ancestral bitch. His bloodline carries through.*

"Then kiss the queen."

He was pleased. *Well now! I have never done that particular magic before.* He came up and gave Jewel a good lick on the face.

"Oh!" she exclaimed, abruptly sitting up. "What's all this slobber on me?"

"I'll explain in a moment," I said. "You were under a sleep spell. A prince kissed you awake. Now we must wake the others."

Soon enough we similarly broke the spells on Myrrh and Nydea, and I introduced Cerberus to them and explained his key role in their release. After a certain initial hesitancy—it would not be politic to call it revulsion—they concluded that they appreciated this. In fact they rather liked the huge canine, and he liked them. There was just something about girls and small-horse-sized dogs. It did not hurt that Myrrh was telepathic, and thus had a strong connection to the mighty carnivore. Nydea was my kind, and able to assume bitch form when she chose, so she also understood.

Then we gathered in a larger cabin for a council of war, sitting cross-legged on the deck, with a single dog's head blissfully on the lap of each maiden, Jewel abstaining because she was at the moment the least virginal of us. I explained as I stroked the master head how the slave girl had turned out to be the Sorceress Medea, and the danger Aladdin and Duban were in. Now we needed to rescue them, with Cerberus' help. He would know the best route. We could take a dhow and portage through the narrowest sections of the cave, then float above and across the River Styx. Getting there was not the problem.

But what would we do once we arrived and encountered the sorceress? We needed to work that out *before* the event. Or else.

CHAPTER SEVENTEEN

The ferry moved steadily over the black water.

Medea of Colchis, daughter of King Aeëtes, niece of Circe, granddaughter of the sun god Helios, and one-time wife to the hero Jason, stood at the prow, hands clasped behind her back, deep in thought.

So far, her plan had worked perfectly.

Too perfectly. True, she had not counted on the arrival of the Flying Dutchman, but upon casting her thoughts over the ship, she had quickly discovered a rather interesting fact. Not only was the King of Aragah on board, King Aladdin, but the legendary sailor, Sinbad, and the clever Thief of Baghdad.

Quite an interesting trio.

With the mighty—and stupid—kraken being cleverly dispatched by a smell potion, of all things, Medea had reached out telepathically, as gods and demigods are wont to do, and made contact with the Thief. The man had been more than accommodating and easily swayed. Promises of fame and riches, along with many nights alone with her, had been enough to get him moving.

Although the monstrous kraken had been thwarted, the beast had caused enough havoc to distract the Sirens long enough for the Thief to gain entrance. The thief who had once before stolen from these very sirens.

Yes, a clever thief indeed.

The invisibility spell that had attached the merchant trader to the hull of the Flying Dutchman itself had been one of her more inspired ideas...and it had worked. The invisible ship had effectively hidden the Thief of Baghdad—and the key to Hades.

Of course, things seemed almost too easy for Medea. That is, until Aladdin's nearly catastrophic mistake. Giving the figurehead the wrong sap from the Tree of Knowledge had nearly ruined everything, especially when the ship sought Allah in the heavens. Only Aladdin's quick thinking with the never-ending story had saved the day. The King of Agrabah was proving to be both a hero—and a royal dolt.

Medea had been forced to strike a deal with the flying ship's accursed captain. She had sensed a coming impasse: with the ship refusing to continue on and Queen Jewel refusing to continue the story.

Medea couldn't have that. She needed the flying ship to both enter the Hinterlands—and to safely escape it. So a deal had been struck with the Captain Figurehead. A deal Medea was bound to. For now. An all-knowledgeable being would have to eventually be disposed of. Such a being would prove problematic in the wrong hands.

For now, though, she needed the ship. That meant getting a quit-claim from Aladdin, as his technical mastery of the ship had not been abated. Only then could she claim its full allegiance.

Behind her, she heard Aladdin mumbling just under his breath, no doubt consulting with the whorish Siren presently residing on his finger as a ring. The ring idea had been a good one, and she was quick to utilize it herself. Now, the famous thief and captain were bound to her, unless the spell was broken. Few would know of the spell, although the young wizard boy might possess such innate knowledge. Yes, the young wizard boy would have to be done away with, too.

She nodded slightly as Charon poled the flat vessel forward, deeper into the dark tunnel. To her right she heard the sounds of another river, this one moving a little faster. This would be the

River Acheron, which converged with the River Styx, all of which led, inevitably, to the Gates of the Underworld.

Charon kept the small vessel steady, expertly poling it over the now slightly-rougher currents of the converging rivers. The tunnel also opened up, and Medea saw they were in another cavern. This one smaller than the other, but with no river bank. Instead, the black water rode up high along the slick, stone walls.

Medea was a woman scorned. She was also a woman betrayed by the man she had loved most, Jason of the Argonauts. Just thinking his name now brought fresh pain to her heart, so much so that she inhaled sharply, breathing in the cool air that swirled above the black waters. She clenched her hands into fists.

She had loved Jason with all her heart, and given him two sons.

And at the thought of her two lost sons, Medea nearly sobbed. But she fought through it. Yes, her sons—murdered by her own hands for reasons that even she didn't fully understand. Medea had gone on an unholy tirade after hearing of her husband's betrayal. She had killed the object of her husband's new love, along with her father. Fearing her own sons would be enslaved for life as punishment for her crimes…Medea had done the unthinkable.

And now she did whimper, so lightly that she was certain no one heard her.

Great gods, had I really killed them? Had I really suffocated my two precious boys?

She had, and there wasn't a day over the many centuries that she hadn't regretted it, hadn't hated herself, hadn't hated Jason all over again for driving her insane with rage.

The ferry picked up speed, and Charon only occasionally poled it forward. Mostly the old ferryman used his long staff to keep the ferry in the center of the river.

But I will not weep another day, she thought. *No, never again.*

Indeed, her plan was genius, and if it worked, Medea would have everything again: her boys and her man. And, with some luck, the entire planet.

The Key to Hades was, in fact, the key. With it, she could see her boys again—and give Jason one last chance at love. And, of course, free the greatest—and most hideous—army the earth had ever seen.

Just as she smiled at that thought, she felt the ferry shift slightly. They were heading toward a rocky shore.

They had reached the Underworld.

CHAPTER EIGHTEEN

They stood on the deck behind the Figurehead, ready to proceed.

"Then we are decided," Nylon said. "We four—" She glanced at Cerberus. "We *five* will proceed in haste to the Gates of Hades and brace Medea before she can actually use the Key to open them. She should not be able to dispatch us when we're all together and fully alert. Duban will throw a devastating stasis spell at her while Cerberus pounces and Aladdin grabs the Key from her neck. Once we have that, she should be relatively powerless."

"'Relatively' remains highly dangerous," Nydea said. "We know of Medea from history. She dates from more than fifteen hundred years ago, and is as cunning and unscrupulous as they come. We may take losses."

"Not nearly as great as the losses we will take if those Gates are thrown open," Jewel said. "It's a risk we have to tolerate. We know that."

The others looked at Myrrh, the youngest by a fair margin. She had been silent. They needed her agreement, so they would know they were unified. She understood this, but had been careful about being too assertive; it was not her place. But now she had to commit openly.

Myrrh took a deep breath. "I am close to Duban," she said. "I can commune mentally with him because he likes me. I can also commune with Aladdin, because he lets me. I will let them know the roles we plan for them, and gain their acquiescence.

But the Sorceress Medea is something else; she has blocked her mind to me throughout. I don't believe she is telepathic herself, but she understands it, and can shield her mind from it. I wish I could know what she is thinking, so she is less of an unknown danger. Without some insight into her thoughts I fear we are on a fool's errand." She smiled weakly. "But yes, I am in, and will do my part."

"You are all fools," the figurehead said scornfully. "You have virtually no idea what you are getting into. But I must admit I have to admire your desperate courage."

"Thank you," Nylon said. "Now I will kiss you farewell." She went forward to do that, while the others boarded a dhow.

"And when we return, I will tell you more tales," Jewel said.

"I will hold you to that, woman."

Nylon delivered her kiss, then joined them in the dhow. "I don't suppose you care to tell us how this will come out?" she called to the figurehead.

"I can't do that."

"Why not, if you know?"

"Because telling you will cause you to change your plan, and then the outcome will also change. It's a paradox. That is the problem with the future; it's fungible."

They ignored that, as none of them knew exactly what the word meant. But Myrrh understood how knowledge of the future could change it, because she had some foretelling ability herself and had run afoul of the effect.

Cerberus was really too big for the dhow, so he elected to run along before it, showing the way.

"Possibly significant point," Nylon said. "The figurehead refused to tell us how our venture would come out, but he did indicate that Jewel would be returning to tell him more tales. That suggests success."

"Not necessarily," Jewel said. "It could mean that I'm the lone survivor."

"Or some other compromise," Nydea said. "The sorceress could enchant you and hold you hostage against Aladdin's cooperation."

"Or that the figurehead was faking it, as he does not know the future," Myrrh said. "If he really knew the future, he'd know how Jewel's stories turn out, and not need her to tell them."

The others nodded soberly. They had no indication at all.

Nylon glanced at Myrrh. "Time for you to tune us out and tune Aladdin and Duban in. We'll shut up and let you focus while we travel."

"Thank you." Myrrh had privately dreaded this moment, because she feared what she would learn. Suppose the situation was already hopeless?

She reached out for Duban. She loved him, and knew he loved her, but they both muted that because the adults thought children were incapable of real love. That made communication at a distance feasible. But some of the thoughts they exchanged would freak out those naive adults.

She connected immediately. *You're awake!* Duban thought.

Awake and well, Myrrh agreed. *Medea put a sleep spell on us, but Queen Nylon returned with Cerberus and woke us.*

But a sleep spell can't be broken with a mere snap of the fingers, he protested. *Medea would not be so careless.*

Cerberus helped, she explained. *Nylon tamed him, and now he is one of us. He has royal ancestry. We are coming to rescue you, but we fear the power of the sorceress.*

I have prepared a mental blast, he thought. *But I am not sure when to use it.*

We are counting on that. We will converge on her as she seeks to use the Key to unlock the Gates of Hades. That should be a fair distraction. Strike then.

I will, he agreed, relieved by the decision.

Now I must contact Aladdin, so he can grab the Key right then.

Duban hesitated. *Myrrh, if things don't work out—*

I love you too, she thought, and sent him a kiss and hug of such nature she could feel his mental blush. Boys were easy to manage, even powerful Magician boys. It would only get easier as she matured physically. Then she moved on to Aladdin. This was more difficult, because he liked her without loving her, a less committed association.

Aladdin, it's Myrrh! Sylvie Siren thought, the first to catch her presence. *I'll enhance the signal.*

Bless the Siren! That would really help.

Myrrh! he thought gladly. *We feared you were—in trouble. When Medea came—*

She put us to sleep. Nylon and Cerberus rescued us.

Cerberus! The Hound of Hades? Nylon diverted him so we could pass.

He is one of us now. Nylon tamed him. We are coming to help you. When Medea tries to use the Key on the Gates, we will attack her in a group, and Duban will blast her mentally. You must grab the Key at that moment, when she is disoriented.

Got it. Thanks. He too was relieved to have a coherent plan of action.

Then on a whim she tried Medea. She had never been able to get into the Sorceress's mind, but if the woman was distracted by her plan to use the Key, she might be careless and Myrrh might be able to sneak in. Anything she learned could be invaluable.

And there she was! The woman was reviewing her life history, as if fearing that it was soon to end. Myrrh tuned in, hiding her presence, because if Medea were to catch on there would be a savage counter-strike. It was as though Myrrh were a fly perched on the woman's head, seeing and hearing without participating.

———

It started, really, with the Golden Fleece.

Two royal Greek children were in danger from their step-mother, who wanted to clear the way for her own child to inherit the kingdom. The children's mother prayed to the god Mercury for assistance, and Mercury sent the winged ram Chrysomallus to carry them to safety. The ram was a wonder to behold, as his fleece was pure gold. He took the children on his back and flew high. But the little girl, Helle, lost her grip, fell off, and drowned in the sea below. Thereafter it was named after her, the Sea of Helle, or the Hellespont. The boy kept his grip and the golden ram carried him to the kingdom of Kolchis, on the Black Sea, ruled by King Aeetes. The king welcomed them, seeing an opportunity here, and so did the king's daughter, Medea, who now had a playmate and a fine pet. But then the boy, in gratitude, sacrificed the ram and gave the Golden Fleece to the king. Medea, mourning the wonderful ram, would have nothing further to do with the boy, and was quietly alienated from her father, who should have prevented the prince from making such a senseless gesture. The ram had performed wonderfully, and been cruelly murdered in return. That was the beginning of Medea's cynicism. Virtue was not necessarily rewarded. She resolved to protect herself by studying sorcery. It turned out that she had a talent for it, and without her father's knowledge she became quite proficient.

Later, when Medea was grown, there came a ship, the Argo, with fifty heroes. The most impressive was the leader, Jason, and because of the intervention of the Goddess Hera she fell in love with him at first sight. She didn't really mind, because she was without a boyfriend and Jason was a truly handsome man. When it turned out that he had come to take the Golden Fleece she saw her chance to accomplish several things at once: punish her father for letting the ram die, win Jason for her own, and keep the fleece close by her so that it could be properly venerated. So when King Aeetes made impossible demands for Jason's possession of the fleece, such as yoking two fire-breathing bulls to plow the field and sow the teeth of a dragon there, which would lead to mischief as the teeth sprouted into warriors who would slay him, Medea met with Jason and helped him. She was of course well familiar with the magic her father was loosing, and knew how to counter it, just in case it would ever be set against *her*. She gave Jason a charm to sprinkle on his body and weapons to make him and them invincible. In return he promised to take her with him when he departed with the fleece, marry her and always love her. She had not at that time learned how to fascinate men without doing favors for them; that would come later.

It worked out exactly as she anticipated. Jason overcame the bulls, yoked them, plowed the field, sowed the dragon's teeth, then following her advice threw a pebble among the resulting warriors. They immediately fell to fighting each other for the worthless bit of stone, and Jason was able to dispatch the few wounded survivors. She also sang to the dragon who guarded the fleece, pacifying it so that Jason could get safely by.

That was just the beginning. Jason did take her with him, did marry her, and had much joy of her magically beautiful body, siring two sons. But complications of politics—doing Jason's bidding she arranged the death of a royal person—they had had to move to Corinth, where Jason deserted her and married the pretty-if-you-like-that-type daughter of the king of Corinth. It seemed there was just something about younger, more virginal princesses that appealed to him. That was when Medea lost it. She sent a poisoned robe to the bride, killing her. Then, fearing that her sons would be vulnerable to retaliation, she reluctantly killed them. Jason, angry for some reason, tried to kill her, and she had to flee to Athens, where, still in her madness, she influenced the king to try to kill the young hero Theseus, the king not knowing that the hero was his son who would inherit what Medea coveted. But the plot was exposed, and Medea had to flee again, this time to Asia, where the land of Media was named after her. But her love for Jason remained, though he was now long dead, and she longed to return to him and perhaps win him back. Thus her present mission to unlock the Gates of Hades. If she could just find Jason there, and reason with him, maybe she could at last achieve the happiness that had eluded her for more than a thousand years. It was the abiding hope that motivated her.

———

Myrrh tuned out, realizing that this so-convenient history meant that the sorceress had known of her intrusion and presented it in an effort to make her case. The irony was that it was effective; Myrrh now understood what motivated Medea, and sympathized. The woman was not evil, merely cruelly battered by fate. She had had to become supremely tough to survive. Why she thought the faithless Jason would make her happy at this late date was a mystery of the foolishness of women. So he was handsome…

Myrrh sighed. Men chose women by their appearance, hardly caring about the content of their character; why not women choosing men similarly? Was Myrrh herself any better? Duban was not bad looking, and he had phenomenal powers of magic, and he was a prince. All good qualifications for an aspiring girl. His music might be considered a waste of time, but she rather liked that too. None of these things reflected firmly on his character. So how could she fault Medea? It was not a question she could answer.

CHAPTER NINETEEN

The ferry lurched slightly as it came to a halt at the river's edge.

Water lapped against the rocks along the banks. I had to admit: I didn't want to get off. I didn't want to face what lay beyond. I wanted to be in my palace, in bed with Jewel, and making deep passionate love. Anywhere but on the banks of the Acheron, the last river into Hades.

Be strong, my liege, whispered Sylvie into my thoughts.

But why has the job of saving the world from the demons of hell fallen upon my shoulders? Surely there is someone more worthy than I. Someone better equipped.

Perhaps, said Sylvie. *Or perhaps not. You have proven yourself uncannily resilient in times of crisis. You are a leader of men. You have perhaps humanity's greatest young wizard on your side. Two of the world's greatest adventurers. A telepathic girl unlike any I have ever seen. And, of course, two nubile nymphs to bring it all together.*

What about Jewel?

She might be our greatest asset.

Why?

Because of your love for her.

I don't understand.

Great love inspires greatness. We are going to need greatness to survive this ordeal, my liege. So please pull it together and get us all out of here.

The nymph's words gave me pause. Put that way, I was ideally equipped to handle the crisis. *But how? What match were we against an angry god?*

We shall see, came Sylvie's reply.

The air was colder here, and would have been devoid of light if not for the torch that flickered near a rocky path. The path led off into a darkness so black that I initially quailed. Anything could be in the darkness.

Not just anything, I thought. *Hades.*

I, of course, came from a different school of thought. One that didn't necessarily believe in Hades, but in a heaven and hell.

Remember, my liege, this is merely a stopover for departed souls, where their lives are reviewed. Those found worthy will go to your idea of heaven. Those found neither good or bad, will end up in a neutral place. And those found lacking will continue on.

Continue on?

Deeper into Hades, my lord. Into what you think of as hell.

I shivered, then thought: *But how does Medea plan to bypass the judges?*

As a goddess, I suspect she knows more about this realm than either of us. We shall have to wait and see.

The three spirits who had been huddled together on the far side of the ferry now drifted past us. One looked back at me, and looked as confused as I felt. I prayed Allah had mercy on his soul. Soon, they had moved past the torch light and faded from view. What lay beyond the darkness, I hadn't a clue.

Medea had gone back to Charon and whispered something into his ear. The ferryman of the dead grinned like a school boy. Medea swept past me and leaped off the ferry to land lithely on the rocks beyond. She held out her hand.

"Come, my lord. Don't look so nervous. We have a dastardly plot to thwart."

Despite myself, I took her hand and was amazed by her strength as she helped me onto the rocky shore. Duban leaped lightly and landed smoothly. Almost instantly, the ferry behind us moved away, and I turned back to watch the old man ease the vessel out onto the swirling black water, leaving us stranded on the bleak shore.

Never had I felt so bereft of hope. I took Duban's hand.

The flickering torch, I saw, wasn't a torch at all. The fire hung suspended in the air. Medea waved her hand and the flame moved before us, lighting the way.

Apparently, the goddess was dispensing with her slave charade. Only a goddess—or one with knowledge of the Underworld— would have known what to do with that flame.

Indeed, sire, said Sylvie. *The child telepath, Myrrh, has informed that Medea had given her access to her thoughts and memories.*

But why?

By revealing sympathetic and, quite frankly, gut-wrenching memories, Myrrh believes the goddess is trying to gain favor with us.

Or gain allies, I thought. *But why go about it like this?*

I suspect she sensed the child telepath poking around, and saw an opportunity. After all, I see no one else here to stop her. Just us.

And if she can win us over...

Nothing will stop her.

I thought about all of this as we moved forward over a smooth, stone trail and through a blackness so deep that it could have been tangible. At any rate, it was oppressive as hell and it played upon old childhood fears of the dark. And why wouldn't it? We were following the very path into the Underworld.

At that moment, I felt a rippling calm course through me, so much so that I immediately suspected the source.

Was that you, Sylvie?

Of course, my liege. We need you calm and alert, not dealing with childhood demons.

Better I deal with real demons, eh? I thought, feeling a euphoria rarely felt outside of a healthy dose of bhang. *But how...*

Easy, my lord. We Sirens have spent an eternity understanding the ways of man. We know the pleasure centers of the brain and how to trigger them gently.

I nearly laughed. In fact, I did. Medea snapped her head around and looked me, her eyes narrowing.

Oops, came Sylvie's words. *A little too much stimulation.*

She corrected her dosage, so to speak, and I soon felt like my old self, minus any fear.

We continued on with Medea leading the way. The flame provided us just enough light to see our feet moving over the flat, smooth path. What lay beyond the light, I hadn't a clue. Maybe demons. Maybe nothing at all. Maybe it was just an eternal darkness, and should one wander off the path, they would forever be lost in darkness. That thought alone would have sent me into a near panic, but now I simply thought and...let it go.

Duban kept close to me, holding my hand tightly, and I realized all over again what a horrible parent I was. Who leads their child into the Underworld?

A parent tasked with saving the world, thought Sylvie.

I nodded at the Siren's words of encouragement, knowing that the Stygian darkness was bringing every old and new fear to the surface of my thoughts.

We continued on, deeper into the darkness, further and further away from the land of the living. To where, I did not know. But I suspected I was about to find out.

"There, father," said Duban, after a short time. Then again, perhaps it had been a very long time. I was only aware of my breathing. And of the flame. And of Medea's perfect backside. And of the darkness. Always the darkness.

I saw it now, too. A light on the far horizon. Or perhaps it was the close horizon. Or perhaps there was no horizon. I'd lost all grasp of self. Of depth. Of the physical world.

Never had I been so grateful to see light.

We continued toward it, over the smooth stone and through the oppressive darkness. Toward the light. The blessed light.

It was another torch.

This time it hovered at head height within a stone cavern with four black tunnels. Where the tunnels led off to, I didn't know, but I could guess.

"The tunnel on the left," said Medea, "leads to the forecourt of the Palace of Hades where the three judges sit, and which newly departed souls must venture." She pointed to the next tunnel. "This tunnel leads to a realm the Christians call Purgatory, but which we call the Fields of Asphodel." She pointed to the next tunnel. "This tunnel here leads to blessed peace—realms of untold beauty and joy."

"And the final tunnel?"

She looked at me. "Hell, of course. Come." And she stepped forward. Into the final tunnel.

The tunnel to hell.

CHAPTER TWENTY

What could I do but follow her?

Some mean-spirited critic inside me suggested that the sight of Medea's supremely evocative rear revived my foolish desire to capture her interest in dalliance. But she was carrying the Key to the Gates of Hades and would use it unless we stopped her. So I had to follow her, didn't I? Anyway, how could we have a grand showdown at the Gates unless we went there?

Both reasons are true, Sylvie thought. *We do need to stop her, and you are foolishly hot for her flesh. Your problem is that you want to accomplish both, and be justified. I don't think that's possible.*

"So we have to go to the Gates," I sub-vocalized.

Well, you could simply try grabbing the key from her neck. That might even work.

No it wouldn't, Myrrh's thought came. *She would stun you the moment you touched her. Stick to the plan.*

"Unless I stunned her first, with a kiss," I retorted. "I just might get both key and body, saving us all much grief."

Medea paused, so that I almost collided with her. Too bad my automatic reflexes averted that. She turned to face me. "But it would be so much fun to try it out," she said.

"What?" I asked, unwilling to believe that she could have read my thoughts.

"I will even give you the Key first," she said, proffering it to me on its chain about her neck. "Kiss me, Aladdin." Somehow her shirt had fallen open under my nose.

107

Don't do it! both Sylvie and Myrrh cried mentally.

Stay out of this, Medea shot back at them, mentally.

Oh, doom! Myrrh thought. *I thought she was not completely telepathic. I was wrong.*

"You were wrong," the sorceress agreed both audibly and mentally. "You are a supremely talented child, but a child nevertheless, lacking experience. I have been on to your plan throughout." She smiled, projecting the image of the expression to Myrrh. "But we have no need to oppose each other. All I want is to recover my beloved Jason from Hades. None of you should object to that. You can become useful allies."

Duban spoke, surprising me. "That is a lie, sorceress. Or at least a mere cover story. You know Jason is not worth your time. He is and always was a shallow cad, deserving only of eternal torment. You want to loose the fiends of Hades on the world, wreaking vengeance on it for making you suffer so long."

Medea took visible stock, appraising the boy. "You are not the mere stripling I took you for. Some day, if you survive, you will be a man to be reckoned with. But as yet you are not. You are young and naive, like Myrrh. Your magic bolt will not stun me; I am shielded against it. You are not prepared for my return thrust. I suggest that you turn around and walk back to the river, where your mother will intercept you and take you home. That will at least save your life, for the time being."

"You can't talk to him that way!" I said angrily. "I'll—"

She turned on me a nonchalant glance that nevertheless invoked my passion full blast. "You will what? Kiss me?"

Don't do it! Sylvie and Myrrh chorused again.

"Why not?" Medea asked them. "I would be satisfied to be Aladdin's mistress."

She would? Now I was really interested.

Fool! Sylvie thought. *She means mistress as in the one who rules, the master, not as in girlfriend. She would be your mistress indeed.*

"Yes, but he would enjoy it, in both senses," Medea said. "At least, for a while." Then she addressed me again. "Take the Key."

I actually started to reach for it, where it hovered on its chain between her superlatively contoured breasts, unable to reach her chest because of the magnitude of the slopes below. But something in her very readiness made me pause. I may be a fool about women, but I also have a certain sense of danger, and I felt it now. "What else does this action imply?"

"Oh, nothing much. Merely that you are freely trading me your authority over the Flying Dutchman for the Key. We will celebrate the exchange with a phenomenal union. You will like that."

So that was it. She was trying to seduce the Dutchman from me, so she could use it to escape once the demons of Hades had been loosed.

"But how can they be loosed if you have the Key?" Medea asked reasonably.

Don't trust her! Sylvie warned.

"But if I have the Key—"

"Don't do it, father," Duban said. "She is more cunning than all of us combined. She has something in mind."

I sighed. They were surely correct. "Some other time," I said, exercising more sheer willpower than I ever could have mustered had my wife's son not been watching me. Of course I loved my wife. Of course I wanted to set a good example for the boy. But had I been alone with this fascinating creature I might have temporarily forgotten these things. Men do.

Men do, Sylvie agreed, relieved.

Medea turned about with a flair of her skirt and resumed her walk down the tunnel. My eyes resumed their analysis of her flexing posterior; they couldn't help it. The skirt seemed translucent. Such a work of erotic art has seldom been crafted in the mortal realm.

"*Never* been crafted," Medea said, annoyed by the slight. She had a case.

The tunnel expanded, becoming a grand gallery. Soon we reached the Gates of Hades. They were impressive. They were set in the wall of the cave, huge ornate curling metallic bars backed by blue screening with the words ABANDON HOPE ALL YE WHO ENTER HERE. In the center was a small access with a keyhole.

Medea turned again to face me. The very cave seemed to pulse for a moment with her beauty, and for a moment I almost lost my balance, as if I had moved without walking. "One more time, Aladdin," she said. "Will you make the trade?"

Give up the ship? I wished there could be some other way. "I don't think so."

"Then it is time for the showdown." Medea took the Key and stepped toward the keyhole.

Then hell, if you will excuse the expression, broke loose. The huge dog Cerberus appeared bounding down the hall, three heads slavering, with a woman riding at the base of each stout neck, and a fourth on the back. They all dropped off and ran toward the sorceress separately, while the dog leaped high into the air, orienting directly on Medea, who paused to face them all.

"Ah, I forgot about the cur," she said, seeming annoyed rather than afraid. "His telepathy cleverly masked their approach. This may be more complicated."

Then Duban loosed his bolt. It was not directed at me, but it felt like an elephant crashing through a stand of bamboo as it passed. It hurtled toward Medea, seeming unstoppable in its horrendous power.

And bounced. It struck Cerberus and hurled him back. It struck the four women and froze them in place. It shoved me like a rogue wave, but I managed to keep my footing. And a back-draft struck Medea and pushed her into the Gate. "Stronger than I thought," she gasped, surprised.

Then the Gate disappeared. It was illusion. Behind it was a gulf, a precipice leading to a drop-off of unfathomable depth. The sorceress had deceived us all. But why?

"The real gate is over here," Medea said, walking back along the gallery. Sure enough, there was a far more modest gate with its own keyhole. It had been covered over by the illusion of a blank wall. The sorceress extended the key toward it, and paused again. "Aladdin, are you sure you won't make the trade? This is your last chance."

She was still willing to give up her mission in order to obtain the flying ship? This did not make complete sense to me. I could not answer immediately.

"No it isn't!" Duban said as he charged toward her. He tackled her around the waist. Both went down in a tangle, and the key flew wide. Toward the gulf.

I leaped toward it. But Jewel was there ahead of me. Only her balance was uncertain, probably from the recent blast, and she was about to go over the edge into the chasm. I was in range to catch the Key or my wife. Not both.

I went for Jewel. I caught her about the waist and hauled her back onto the firm cave floor. As I did so I saw, mostly peripherally, Cerberus going for the Key. One head caught it. And inadvertently swallowed it. Then the big dog's inertia carried him on over the brink, and he dropped out of sight. Oh, no!

I'm all right, Cerberus thought. *I can handle drops. But it will take me a while to climb out of this pit, and longer to get the Key out.*

"You should have let me go," Jewel said. "I could have handled the drop too."

"No!" I said, horrified by the thought.

Then her features changed. "Because I'm not your wife. I'm Nylon. I assumed her likeness in case the sorceress tried to kill her so as to put pressure on you. Put me on your finger and go to Jewel." She shrank as she spoke, and in a moment was back on my finger.

"And of course you are too late," Medea said, extricating herself from Duban's grasp. "I made sure of that. I unlocked the real Gate before showing you the fake, so I could have more time to tempt you with the Key. Now it's show time." She flung open the smaller Gate.

I charged her and Duban grabbed for her. We met in a tangle of arms, legs, and torsos that crashed though the Gate. But I kept my focus on what counted: I reached out and slammed the Gate shut behind us. That would keep the demons confined.

Good show, Sylvie thought. *Now how do we get out, without the Key?*

Then I realized: I had shut the gate behind us, locking us in. "Good question," I said as I unstuck my face from a remarkable bosom and Duban escaped the scissor grip of a marvelous pair of legs. "I will get back to you on that."

"We have a more immediate problem," Medea said, putting herself back together. "The fiends of Hades have arrived. I think we have become accidental allies."

We looked up. What appeared to be a storm of sheer awfulness was about to engulf us. We did indeed have a problem.

CHAPTER TWENTY-ONE

*I*s *there a way to fight back, Nylon?* I asked, even as the dense cloud of awfulness coalesced into many hundreds of winged demons. No, many thousands. Each had flat faces, black eyes, clawed talons and wings like dragons.

We are in their realm, Aladdin. Here, demons have free rein. Here, there is no hope. Perhaps for all eternity. We are beyond even mortal prayers to the gods.

And yet, we had one such god in our presence. A demigod, granted, but a god nonetheless. Medea, of course, was picking up my thoughts. She said, "Hades delights in torturing my kind as surely as he does your kind. We are doomed. We were supposed to free the demons of hell, Aladdin, not get locked inside with them."

Don't listen to her, my liege, came Myrrh's faint but urgent voice in my head. She was shielding her thoughts, directing them only at me, in a way I never fully understood but seemed to be second nature to her. *She's hatching a nefarious plan.*

What kind of plan?

Myrrh paused, even as the demons continued to gather above us. Now they were swirling slowly. As they did, I scanned our surroundings for the first time. Before us, black rock stretched as far as the eye could see, glowing intermittently. It turned out that all the childhood stories I'd heard of the place were true, and I had no doubt that the glowing rocks were, in fact, tunnels that led to the fires of hell.

I'm doing my best to poke around without her knowledge. Luckily, she's distracted by the demons and fears for her own immortal soul. But I think I have a handle on her plan.

Which is?

She plans to use Sinbad and the Thief in exchange for her husband, Jason.

What about her two sons?

Her sons are not in hell. They are in Purgatory. At least, that's what she believes. Myrrh paused again, and I knew she was probing the demigod's mind. *She's aware that her plan may not work. Apparently, Hades is unpredictable at best, and the supreme ruler of the Underworld. Obviously, he makes the rules. Not a lesser god.*

Does she have plans for me?

For now, she desires to return to the mortal world with you.

What about Jason?

With both of you. She is, after all, the goddess of lust, Aladdin. She can more than accommodate the two of you.

Her plans for me were not important. At least, not at the moment. Escaping with Duban, Sinbad, the Thief and the nymphs was my primary objective.

I sensed Queen Nylon and Sylvie closely following my train of thoughts. I also sensed something else from the two bound nymphs: fear. I didn't blame them.

From above a demon screeched, and now they all screeched, their mouths stretching wide, showing long teeth. My bowels instantly turned to water.

Allah be with me, I thought.

Just then a winged creature dropped from the sky, landing directly in front of us with such force that the rocky earth shook. The creature straightened slowly and its black wings folded in on themselves smoothly.

The demon was tall and thin and looked very different than the demon I had seen in Djinnland. Perhaps that demon had been native to that world. Or perhaps there were varying degrees of hideousness. I could imagine no creature looking more foul than the one moving towards us now.

"Seven unexpected arrivals," it said, and although the entity spoke in a whisper, its voice carried easily. "Master will be pleased."

Above, the demons continued to circle and swirl. Sometimes they dipped closer, hissing and flapping their wings. Mostly, they seemed to be waiting and watching.

Medea stepped boldly forward. "Tell Lord Hades that Medea is here to see him and to offer him a trade."

The entity came closer, its clawed feet clicking over the smooth stone. Its black flesh undulated with the motion, the long strips of muscle flexing. I shivered. Duban hugged my leg tightly. He was, after all, still a boy. And I was still the worst father ever.

"A trade?" whispered the demon. "The master does not trade. The master takes what he wants."

"I understand that," said Medea, folding her arms under her ample bosom. "But he might be pleased to know that Medea, Goddess of Lust, is here."

The demon turned its flat face to the side, so much so that I thought its head would twist off. "Yes, I imagine master will be very pleased to have the…goddess of lust as his eternal slave."

Medea clearly didn't like the sound of that. She had been about to speak, but paused instead. However, she quickly collected herself. "Obviously, Lord Hades takes what he wants, when he wants here in his realm. I am only asking for an audience."

"Master doesn't take audience with the damned."

"Technically," said Medea, clearly thinking fast, "we are not damned. We are of the living, and should, therefore, be given a special audience with Hades."

"Ah, yes. The living," said the creature, and now he stepped closer still and dipped his flat face down toward me and studied me with his round, black eyes. My bladder threatened to spill.

Never had I seen something so hideous at such close proximity. "Well, we have ways of taking care of the living here."

"I have no doubt," said Medea. "But first an audience with Hades. Then do what you must."

The demon paused in his examination of me to look back at Medea. "You are a persistent wench. Very well, I shall inquire if master will see you. It's not often we see the living in our realm. He might have some special, ah, plans for you. Plans for your deaths no doubt."

The demon then flicked his hand once and three more demons descended from the sky, each grabbing one of us under the arms and lifting us into the air.

Aladdin! came Myrrh's frantic voice. No doubt she had seen all of this through my eyes. *What do we do?*

Her voice growing fainter as we climbed higher into the black sky. Duban hung from the demon's claws next to me, as did Medea.

Just get the key and be ready to unlock the gate.

What about you? she asked, although her words were only mere whispers in my thoughts.

I'm going to figure a way out of this mess, I thought, but wondered if my words had reached the girl. After all, we had finished climbing and were now speeding rapidly through the empty skies above Hell, and toward a palace that sat high upon a steep rocky hill.

This should get interesting.

CHAPTER TWENTY-TWO

The scenery below changed.

Now I saw a golden river coursing between snow-capped mountains, with people disporting themselves along its banks. How could such a nice scene be here in hell? I could see that Duban and Medea were similarly curious.

"Show them," the lead demon said.

The minions descended until we were flying close enough to get a better view. It was horrible. The river was not golden so much as a coursing flow of fire, liquid lava from some volcano, burning everything it touched. The men were not enjoying themselves so much as trying to cross that flow, burning their toes. Why? Because on the other side were clusters of luscious nude damsels eagerly beckoning them.

"They are wracked with thirst," the demon explained helpfully. "So they eat of the snow of the mountains, freezing their faces. But when it finally melts, it is not water but lust-inciting wine that makes them utterly desperate for the company of obliging maidens. But first they must cross the river of fire. They are already dead, so it can't kill them, but it does make them hurt as much as it would mortal folk. That makes crossing difficult."

"What a sublime torture!" Medea said appreciatively. "Men deserve it."

"It works on women too, cute buns," the demon said. "They become as charged as the men. But they too must cross the fire, and suffer similarly. And of course when they do navigate the

117

river and reach the handsome beckoning men, the men change their minds and ignore them. They are of course mere demons emulating human folk."

Medea frowned. Evidently she did not find that as amusing.

We flew on, seeing other torture settings of all kinds, ranging from standard torture chambers to innovative vivisection. It was like looking at a crowded city from above; each section had its own specialty, but the suffering was universal. Hell was not a nice place.

We came to a giant castle girt with flying flags. But closer up we saw that the flags were not cloth, but impaled people struggling desperately to get free but only making their condition worse. Some were men, some were women, and some were children. The din of their screaming was uncomfortable.

"Everybody suffers," the demon said with satisfaction. "Including the spectators."

We swooped into the main access and through the long passages. There were murals depicting further tortures. Then I realized that these were not paintings, but condensed scenes of actual events; the victims were moaning and bleeding.

Then we were in the main audience hall, standing, the minions gone. There was Lord Hades, seated on a throne carved from a giant skull. "Welcome to Hades," he said. "King Aladdin, Magician Duban, Sorceress Medea, and four others on your fingers. We seldom are visited by mortals who remain alive. To what do I owe the dubious pleasure of this visit?"

Sylvie and Nylon, on my fingers, were silent, not wishing to call any avoidable attention to themselves. I suspected the same was true of Sinbad and the Thief, on Medea's fingers.

"I came to proffer a deal," Medea said.

Hades eyed her. I saw her clothing become transparent wherever his gaze progressed. Had any of her assets been false, as is the case with some women, they would have been exposed. "I am more than surfeit with experienced women."

"But not with mortal ones," Medea said. "All your whores are long since dead, however they may appear."

"True. I long for mortality and inexperience. There is precious little naivete here, and that is highly perishable." He seemed sad for a moment. "But let me hear you out, sorceress. What is the deal you propose?"

"I will trade Sinbad the Sailor and the Thief of Baghdad for my beloved Jason. It is a good deal for you, as both are mortal while Jason is not."

I saw the rings on her fingers twitch: the two named men were objecting. Not that she cared.

"I am intrigued," Hades said. I had the feeling that he was playing cat and mouse with her, one of the very few males who could. What was he up to?

"And I want to take Aladdin back with me, as my second love slave," Medea said.

Hades glanced at me. "Is Aladdin not married, and with a competent concubine he wraps around his finger?"

Ouch.

"What of it?"

Ouch again. Neither of those two gave half a rotten fig for our sentiments.

Hades smiled. "You might after all be fun to play with, sorceress. But I am jaded. It will be more entertaining to douse you in honey and chain you out for the ants to eat. After the first century I will think of something else to do with you."

"Then consider my second offer. You like virginal mortals? These days no girl over thirteen will qualify, nor would she come to you if she did. But there is one who would."

I felt an ugly chill. Where was Medea going with this?

"Who? Speak, woman, while you still have a tongue."

"Her name is Myrrh. Not only is she young, pretty, and physically innocent, she is telepathic. You would find her completely delightful."

"No!" Duban and I said almost together before Medea even completed her speech, and there was a surge of outrage from Myrrh herself. I had thought she was now out of range, but maybe not quite.

"Unfortunately that particular mortal girl was caught on the wrong side of the Gate," Hades said. "I could not summon her, regardless, as I lack power over the mortal realm, and she would not come to me voluntarily. She is not yours to bargain with."

"You have but to threaten to torture Duban, here, and she will make the deal immediately to spare him."

Hades considered. "True?" he asked Myrrh.

"No!" Duban said.

I felt the horror and the tears as Myrrh answered. *True.* She was young, but she truly loved Duban.

And of course the Lord of Hades would do it, in his utter cynicism, to win his innocent mortal victim. Myrrh would do it to save Duban. Medea knew this, and so did Hades. Now we knew why the sorceress had communed with Myrrh: to get her measure.

"Perhaps we do have a deal," Hades said. "But there remain some trifling details." He snapped his fingers. "Jason."

Jason appeared. He was a handsome man in Greek attire. "Master."

"Your ex-wife Medea wishes to take you with her to the mortal realm. Do you care to go?"

"She killed my beloved!" Jason said. "And my children. Bring her here so I can torture her myself."

Hades glanced at Medea, amused. "It seems he spurns you again, sorceress."

"Bind him to me," Medea said evenly. "I don't want him as an independent man; I want him as my obedient love slave. The same way I want Aladdin. They can both curse me as long as they satisfy my lust."

"I wouldn't touch you, granddaughter of a dog!" Jason swore. "Except to whip your sorry hide."

"There may be whipping, yes," the sorceress murmured. "But not of that nature." She licked her lips.

Now I knew the nature of Medea's interest in me. It was a turnoff, quite apart from my loyalty to Jewel and Nylon.

Thank you, Nylon thought.

"Since the group of you entered my domain voluntarily, you are in my power," Hades said. "So it seems the deal is mine to make. The three of you and the two female rings will be freed unharmed, Jason the Greek will be bound to Medea, and the girl Myrrh will meet you at the gate and enter in your place." He glanced at Medea. "Satisfactory, canine granddaughter?"

Medea opened her mouth, but I spoke first. "No!"

Hades glanced at me with mild curiosity. "You are under the impression that you have some say in this matter?"

"I demand that we settle this in another manner," I said. "As is the right of kings."

"And this manner is?"

"Trial by personal combat, me versus you, with scimitars."

"Now this is really interesting," Hades said, not at all fazed. "A good individual combat for high stakes is always entertaining. The minions of hell will enjoy the spectacle. But we will need two things."

"Seconds," I said immediately. "To make sure the sides are fair and there is no cheating. Duban will be mine."

"Of course. I will take as my second—" He paused. "Medea."

The sorceress was startled. "We are not on the same side!"

"We don't need to be, granddaughter. You just need to do the best job you can."

She considered. "I—suppose so. There is precedent."

"What is the other thing?" I asked suspiciously.

"We need to redefine the terms. If you win, all of you go free and Medea gets Jason too. If I win, I get Myrrh—and Medea. As my love slaves."

"How can I second you when I don't want to be your love slave?" Medea demanded.

Hades stroked his beard. "I suppose that is a problem. Also, the sides would be unfair, as you have considerably more experience in sorcery than the boy does. But there is a simple fix for both problems."

I *really* did not trust this. "What fix?"

"We will exchange seconds. Medea will support you, and the boy will second me. He is honest, so will do his best in that temporary role. That will make the sides approximately even. Agreed?"

I opened my mouth to protest, but could not think of anything effective to say.

"Agreed," Medea said.

Agreed, Myrrh thought.

"Agreed," Duban said. That last surprised me most.

A circular arena formed around us. A huge audience of demons and damned souls was already in place. It seemed the fight was on.

CHAPTER TWENTY-THREE

"However," Hades said, "You neglected a detail. You, as the challenger, have the right to combat. I, as the challenged, have the right to select the weapons."

He was right. I nodded, grimly.

"And I may elect to take more than the two mistresses. To the victor belong the spoils, as someone will sometime say."

I did not answer. This was his domain. He could cheat if he wanted to. But that meant that I could in turn modify a term or two of the deal if I discovered a way to do it. Small comfort at the moment, but it just might make a difference.

Hades summoned one of his lesser demons.

At least, I assumed it was lesser since it was a good deal shorter than the winged monstrosities who flew us to Hades' palace. It approached Hades cautiously, and I soon saw why: in a blink of an eye, a fiery sword appeared in the god's hand. The sword flashed and the head of the demon promptly fell free. Hades caught it neatly and dropped it into a sack that next magically appeared in his hand. He casually tied it off as other demons dragged the headless body away. I couldn't help but notice that the head in the bag was cursing and spitting and trying its best to use its horns to gouge the hand that held it.

"Our ball," said Hades, flipping the sack up and catching it.

I was aware of running contests, archery contests, wrestling contests and mock battle contests, but never one that involved a "ball." Balls, usually made up of rubber from trees and imported into my kingdom, were for kids to play with. To roll around and kick. Not for adult games.

"What do you propose?" I asked, as the "ball" continued snapping and snarling inside the bag.

Hades motioned to a stone hoop hanging vertically from inside the arena. "The rule is simple, King Aladdin. The ball must travel through the hoop five times. The first to do so wins."

"You are a powerful god," I said. "I hardly see how this is fair."

"I'm not known for fairness, but I do have, let's say, a competitive streak. Very well, the arena will be magic-free." Just as Hades spoke these words, Duban and Medea disappeared. When I blinked and looked again, they had reappeared opposite each other just outside of the arena. Hades continued, "Only our seconds can perform magic on our behalf. Your son for me. Medea for you."

"And if I win?"

"You won't, but if, by some strange fluke, that you do, then I will grant you your freedom. Oh, and let's relieve you of your nymphs, too." He snapped his fingers and the rings disappeared from my hand, to reappear as Sylvie and Nylon standing next to Medea.

With the removal of the nymphs, my telepathy also disappeared, and for the first time in a long, long time, I felt truly alone.

Not entirely alone, came Myrrh's words. *I'm still here. Hades has no control over me. At least, not yet.*

I understood the implication in her words. It was up to me...and perhaps Medea, to somehow defeat the ruler of the Underworld in a game I was unfamiliar with, while opposing my own highly gifted son.

I will do my best, Myrrh, I thought back. *Or die trying.*

She seemed touched by my sentiments. She paused, collected herself, then added: *And if need be, my liege, I can relay Nylon's, Sylvie's or even Jewel's thoughts.*

I nodded. That could be helpful, but I suspected that I was going to have to rely on my own wiles and athleticism here, limited as they might be. Despite what my wife might think of me, I had always been a fleet-footed scamp, well before my days of discovering the magical lamp. Back when I had to rely on my street smarts and quick feet.

Hades next dropped the snarling ball in the dirt and ordered us to march off twenty steps. Demons of all shapes and sizes swirled around the arena, flitting between the humans who were chained together. All watching the spectacle below. All watching me take on the God of the Underworld.

Hades was still a head taller than me—and nearly twice as wide. A formidable foe by any right. And as the chanting began in the crowd—a combination of hissing and shrieks—Hades gave me a wicked grin, then dashed forward. Toward the demon head. The ball.

The game had begun.

———

"It's begun," Myrrh reported to the others. She was leaning against the gate, her forehead pressed into the cold iron. She was seeing through Aladdin's eyes, and it wasn't pretty. "It's a ball game to five, and Aladdin is already down two to nothing."

"Oh, camel dung," said Jewel. "And what of Duban?"

"He's secretly being controlled by Hades. The god of the Underworld is far too clever. Or thinks he is. He's taken over Duban's will, forcing him to fight against his father. Worse, he's tapped into Duban's latent talents, and is utilizing them in ways that Duban never thought possible. In effect, he just turned our boy into a world-class wizard, of the likes few have ever seen."

Jewel paced before the great iron gate, running her hand through her hair. She was having trouble wrapping her brain around the fact that her only son was currently in hell, being manipulated by Hades himself, in a fight—if not to the death, then for all eternity.

"Aladdin has been sitting on the throne for far too many years to outplay Hades," she said. "We're going to have to bring in some reinforcements."

"But who?" Myrrh was presently too distracted by the demented ball game to telepathically see where Jewel was going with this.

For an answer, Jewel stopped pacing and removed an amulet from around her neck. To most, it appeared to be just another royal emerald of spectacular size and shape. But Jewel knew differently.

When they departed the magical Kingdom of Djinnland, King Lamprey—the djinn who was once trapped in Aladdin's lamp—had presented her with the gift...and instructions.

She recalled the instructions now, and rubbed the massive amulet three times. To her shock, although she really shouldn't have been shocked, a deep male voice suddenly spoke from behind her.

"Queen Jewel, it's a pleasure seeing you again."

She gasped and turned, and so did Myrrh. "Lamprey!" said Jewel. "You came."

Lamprey bowed slightly. "Of course, my lady. Aladdin gave me back my kingdom. I am bound to him now through the heart." Next the powerful djinn took in his surroundings. "Aw, I see our favorite king has found a way to get himself into even more mischief. May I presume he's behind this gate to hell?"

"Yes, playing a ballgame with Hades himself."

"And let me guess: his immortal soul is at stake?"

"Yes. His among many others."

The djinn looked over at the girl. "And what's the score, Myrrh?"

"It's presently three to nothing. Aladdin is taking a beating."

Lamprey nodded. "And who has the key to the gate?"

"It's with Cerberus. One of the heads swallowed it."

"Of course," said Lamprey, laughing. "And where is that old dog?"

"Down here, my lord," barked the beast, his telepathy carrying the meaning.

Lamprey leaned over the edge and chuckled to himself, then looked back at Jewel. "It appears that you summoned me just in time," he said. "Besides, I have an old score to settle with the god of the Underworld."

"An old score?"

"The old devil caused much mischief in Djinnland, a land where he was not welcome. Now, let's fetch this key and save Aladdin."

CHAPTER TWENTY-FOUR

"**B**ut is this legitimate?" Jewel asked. "Isn't it supposed to be just the two of them as prizes, Myrrh and Medea?"

"It was, but Hades modified the rules," Lamprey said. "That, by the divine order of things, is a tort, and Aladdin now may similarly modify them. Technically he needs to request my support." He glanced at Myrrh, who closed her eyes, focusing.

"A what?" Jewel asked. "I am not familiar with this tortoise."

"A tort. A wrongful act apart from breach of contract," Lamprey explained. "Such as a pie maker not being allowed to pee in the pie even if the customer did not think to request that it be pure."

Jewel nodded appreciatively. "Hades peed in Aladdin's pie by changing the stakes of the contest. It was supposed to be just Myrrh and Medea as mistresses, not the whole lot of us."

"Exactly. The Lord of Hades has gotten away with arrogance for too long there in his subterranean kingdom, and thinks he can ignore the fundamental rules of honor combat. We shall re-educate him."

"I have informed Aladdin," Myrrh reported. "He formally requests your support."

"That will do," Lamprey said. "The background conventions have been honored." He flew down into the gulf, picked up huge Cerberus with no seeming effort, and carried him back to the upper level. The dog seemed satisfied to be carried; obviously the two had met before, and respected each other.

"But the key won't come out for days," Jewel said, eyeing the big body.

"With your permission, friend," Lamprey said to the dog.

Cerberus opened the mouth of the head that had swallowed the Key. Lamprey put a hand in, and reached on down inside the dog's throat, all the way to his stomach. In a moment he pulled it out again, holding the Key. It dripped with digestive juices, but was intact. Lamprey tapped the nearby wall, a jet of clear water came out, and he rinsed the Key and handed it to Jewel with a small flourish. The little fountain ceased.

"Thank you," she said, pretending this was routine. "So now we can get in. What then? I doubt we can reach Aladdin fast enough to save him."

"We won't save him," Lamprey said. "We won't even be on the scene. He will save himself. We have but to be inside Hades so that we are in the same venue. The demons will not be paying attention. It will be a picnic." He smiled. "Complete with sandwiches."

"With what?"

"They may not have been invented in this period. But who's counting?" A big hamper appeared in his hands, overflowing with choice morsels and beverages.

Jewel did not argue the case. She put the Key to the lock, turned it, and the Gate opened. They entered as a group: Lamprey, Jewel, Myrrh, Cerberus, and Nydea.

Inside was a rather pleasant landscape. They were in a clearing in a forest, the ground covered by very short thick grass. "The default state," Lamprey explained. "When the demons are not focusing on making it horrible. They wile away the dull hours by playing golf. It provides them practice with their vilest language."

"Playing in the gulf?"

"Golf. A decadent western sport, not yet invented, that men love, consisting of using sticks to knock little balls into holes."

"Isn't that like sex?" Nydea asked, smiling.

"Close enough. Now have your picnic while I focus on Aladdin. He is behind four to nothing, so it is time. Myrrh, get back in touch. Time is brief."

"Do that," Jewel agreed as she and Nydea unpacked the hamper. Cerberus joyfully went to pay homage to the nice tree trunks.

I was behind four to nothing. One more point and I would be done for. I had no idea what to do, as I was hopelessly clumsy at this crazy game.

Aladdin. It was Myrrh's thought, much stronger and clearer than before. *You must do a conversion. Open your mind to me so I can channel it.*

I did not argue. I trusted her. I opened my mind.

Something poured in. Not information, but technique. The conversion was from scimitar wielding, which I well knew how to do, to basketball, which was hopelessly strange. I was amazed.

I had the ball, which was still cursing and snapping. It was a rule of this game that the side that scored had to give the ball to the other side, at least for a while. I had been wary of the ball's vicious teeth, but now I simply smacked it on the mouth, hard enough to shut it up. Then I advanced on the high basket, bouncing the ball repeatedly on the floor by boxing its ears. This was akin to approaching my opponent with my sword ready. The ball was so stunned it dribbled.

Hades intercepted me, reaching out to take the ball from me as he had readily done before. I parried, not by clanging my blade against his blade, but by shielding the ball with my shoulder so that his hand smacked me instead of the ball, knocking me down.

"Foul!" the referee called. Hades looked surprised; hitherto the fouls had all been mine, giving him free shots at the hoop. This time the free throw was mine.

I stood before the hoop, which looked impossibly high above my head, and casually flung the ball toward it, translating a demonstration scimitar thrust. It sailed up high, then dropped neatly through the hoop. I did know how to thrust.

"Lucky foul," Hades said. "Lucky shot."

I did not argue the case. The longer he overlooked my sudden proficiency, the better for me.

Now he had the ball again, and I had to intercept him. He bounced the ball toward the hoop, disdaining even to guard against me, such was the contempt in which he held me. The ball was bouncing so hard that its dribbling was worse; spit fairly flew. I thrust my point right toward Hades' gut, only translating it to my hand sweeping rapidly inside to catch the ball just before it reached his hand. In effect I had disarmed him, forcing the scimitar from his grip. I bounced it to the side, keeping up with it. I ran around him as he stood amazed, circled, and dribbled up to the hoop. I flung the ball up in another scimitar flourish, and it passed through the hoop for my second score. Four to Two.

Hades took the ball and charged me. Good; I had made him mad. I stepped back as if to get out of his way, then suddenly dived at his huge legs, catching the ball on the way. Hades grabbed for me, but I was already passing under his body, bouncing the ball. I came out behind him, turned, and flung the ball far down toward the basket. Such was my skill with the scimitar that even from that long distance it scored, glancing off the stone before passing through. Four to Three.

Hades' complexion darkened. He took the ball, but this time focused on me. Something flicked toward me—and bounced in a splay of light.

Hades whirled, furious, looking to the side. There was Medea, her own hand raised in a magic gesture. "Magic is forbidden," she called. "As Aladdin's second, I blocked your bolt. Try it again and you're disqualified."

Hades looked ready to explode. But his own second, Duban, nodded. "Do not disqualify yourself," he called. "Lest you forfeit the match. Calm yourself and play conservatively. You still have the advantage."

What could he do? His second was giving him excellent advice. Hades focused on the ball and charged forward again.

And I dodged aside and let him pass, evading his scimitar. Only to sneak my hand in as he passed and push the ball to the far side, never touching his flesh. Then I scooted around, caught the ball, and made another marvelous fling to the hoop. Swish, and it passed through. Four to Four.

Hades took the ball. "I don't know how you so suddenly became adept," he said. "But now I have seen your tricks and I will not be falling for them again. I am going to score." And he dribbled determinedly forward.

I knew I could not match him in straight skill. He had reach and power, and now that he was alert, he would not be careless. What was I to do?

CHAPTER TWENTY-FIVE

I stood beneath the stone vertical hoop as Hades bore down on me. He lowered his shoulder and kept the demon head ball near his hip, shielded from me. There was no stealing the ball this time.

What to do? In battle, I would normally use an enemy opponent's weight against him—first parrying a sword strike, then dropping a shoulder and heaving him over me.

I knew such an act would result in a foul, and give the god a free shot at the hoop.

He continued toward me, simultaneously grinning and grimacing. He knew how to play this game. He knew he had me. One shot and it was over. For all eternity.

Be still, Aladdin, came Myrrh's words.

Be still? I thought. *He'll run me over!*

Precisely.

I was suddenly certain the familiar single word that appeared in my thoughts hadn't been from Myrrh. In fact, I was suddenly certain it was from—no, was it possible?

Anything is possible, my good friend, came Lamprey's words, relayed from Myrrh.

Lamprey!

But of course—

But how?

Nevermind that now. Be still, Aladdin.

I don't understand.

You will.

But as Hades continued to bear down on me, I suddenly saw the logic. This was a game. Not hand-to-hand combat. And in a game, I doubted one's opponent could simply run another opponent over. It would be a foul. One was given the right to stand one's ground. And Hades, I was certain, was assuming I would leap out of his way, or foul him going for the ball. I doubted he would expect me to stand my ground.

And so that's exactly what I did. Both feet planted shoulder width. Hades dropped his shoulder still, and came at me even faster. He sought to intimidate me. I was intimidated, trust me. Who wanted such a Goliath of a being to run over them? Not me.

Be strong, Aladdin.

I held my ground and a moment later, Hades drove his shoulder into my chest, leveling me and knocking the wind out of me. I caught his expression just as contact was made: one of utter surprise.

"Foul!" he cried.

"Precisely," said the referee. "Aladdin of Agrabah is awarded one free shot."

I took my position at the appropriate free shot line. Above and around me, demons hissed. Hades glared at me. I swallowed, wishing like hell that this ball was, instead, a bow and arrow and I was aiming instead at a bullseye. From here, the vertical loop seemed impossibly small, but I knew no magic could help.

The snapping ball didn't help. I hefted it in my hands, getting a feel for the weight. It was now or never.

I raised the demon-head ball, took aim.

The ground began to shake. A thundering sound appeared to my right. I turned. Something massive was bearing down on me. A beast of some kind with a thick horn protruding from between its eyes and a smaller one beneath. It was covered in body armor and it was moving mind-bogglingly fast.

From the outside of the arena, I saw Duban with his eyes closed and hands raised. The creature had been summoned by him. My own stepson.

Unlike Hades, there was no surviving this charge. I was about to be flattened—that is, until a massive hole appeared in the dirt of the arena, and the charging beast promptly dropped from sight.

I was just breathing a sigh of relief when a shadow passed overhead. No, not a winged demon. Something bigger. I looked up as a dragon bore down on me. Black talons extended. Hades chuckled nearby. In the next moment, another creature appeared behind the first, descending fast. Another dragon—but bigger. The two winged creatures battled in mid-air, exchanging blasts of fire that seared the air just above my head and obliterated a whole section of shrieking demons.

Now the dragons were locked talon to talon, circling in the air, where they disappeared with a thunderous crash beyond the arena.

Shoot the ball, Aladdin, came Lamprey's words. *Now.*

I nodded and swallowed and had just turned back to the vertical stone rim when I heard something hissing nearby. It was a snake. I was sure of it, and it was bearing down on me.

Focus, Aladdin.

Except I wasn't sure whose words those were. Maybe my own. I did focus, doing my best to blot out the slithering form that was rapidly appearing in my peripheral vision, and shot the ball—

It sailed up and toward the hoop.

My shot looked good. The ball had a nice arc to it. I had lined it up nicely. Perhaps my eternal soul would be saved after all…

And as the ball approached the rim, I saw something that made me blink hard. The basket shifted slightly to the left. Just slightly. The demon-head ball clanked off the stone and fell with a thud. No one could have noticed it but me.

"And me," said Lamprey, but now the powerful djinn wasn't in my head. He was by my side. And with a swipe of his hand, the massive snake, surely big enough to swallow me whole, exploded into tens of thousands of earth worms, which quickly burrowed into the dirt of the stadium. The djinn turned to Hades. "No magic, old friend. You are disqualified."

Hades, perhaps for the first time since I had set eyes on the god of the Underworld, looked truly surprised. "I should have known Aladdin would bring his pet djinn."

"I'm quite a pet," said Lamprey, and raised his hands and an explosion unlike anything I had ever heard rocked the arena and sent the god of the Underworld hurling back. Lamprey next turned to me. "Aladdin, I suggest you run. Take your boy and nymphs and leave. I have an old score to settle here, and it will not be pretty—or safe—for you to hang around."

Can you teleport all of them back to the gate? asked Myrrh frantically, her words appearing in my mind and no doubt Lamprey's.

"No," came Lamprey's verbal reply, as he turned to face Hades who was just now picking himself up. "It takes far too much concentration—and I'm a little distracted right now."

Demons erupted everywhere, filling the sky, shrieking and swooping. Damned humans scattered in every direction, many breaking free of their chains. The round arena began collapsing, but I wondered just how real it was. Medea was gone. Where she had gone off to, I hadn't a clue. Duban and the nymphs were soon at my side.

Duban threw his arms around my waist. "Father, it wasn't me—"

"I know—"

In that moment, an explosion from Hades rocked us, hurling us off our feet. As I sat up, I saw that Lamprey had protected us with something that looked very much like a shield of light. Hades moved toward us determinedly. Many of his most powerful demons had stopped swooping and appeared behind him or at his side, each more hideous-looking than the next. And all that stood between them and us was Lamprey, King of Djinnland.

To my surprise, Lamprey called the boy over and spoke to him quietly, although he kept his eyes on the approaching horde from hell. My stepson nodded solemnly. "Now go," said Lamprey. "Hurry."

"What about you?" I asked. There was no way in hell—literally—I was going to leave my friend alone.

"I'll be fine, my friend. Trust me. I've been waiting for this moment for a long, long time."

Just then, more beings appeared around Lamprey, at first dozens of them…and then hundreds, thousands. Djinns. All of them. Lamprey's army.

Now Lamprey looked back at me and winked. "Remember, Aladdin, trust the boy."

I took Duban's hand and summoned the nymphs to my fingers. Soon, we were dashing away, back through the crumbling arena and out into an open field—and then plunging into a dense forest.

CHAPTER TWENTY-SIX

We hardly got into the forest before we encountered Medea. "Beware," Duban said. "She is no longer your second."

Excellent advice, Nylon thought, and Sylvie agreed. They did not much like the sorceress.

"No longer," Medea agreed. "Nor are you Hades' second, Duban. But we retain a common interest: to get out of Hades. I want to establish a truce until we accomplish that."

I pondered quickly. Medea had been an excellent second during my combat with Hades, and she could surely help us escape this dangerous realm.

Also, you still want to get into her pantaloons, Nylon thought.

I turned to Duban. "What do you think?"

The boy appraised the woman with the attitude of someone who no longer feared her power. Knowing Duban, I suspected that was justified; he had evidently learned a lot of magic in a hurry. "If she commits to a truce, she will keep it," Duban said. "It is better to have her with us than against us."

Oh, fish dung! Sylvie thought. *You will get into her pants.*

There's no accounting for a man's tastes, Nylon agreed.

I did not argue that case. "Truce," I agreed.

Medea stepped forward and kissed me. This time it was not an attempt to sexually enslave me, but more of a promise to be honored in due course. I was quite pleased to have it.

"As your ally in truce," Medea said, "I must warn you: do not proceed farther into this forest. I came out here to explore the way back to the Gates, and ascertained that this is the Lost Forest. No one who enters it can find his way out of it, until summoned by the ruler of Hades. It is where souls are parked until Hades decides how best to torture them. It is not unpleasant, but it is a prison. We must find another route."

Duban nodded. "I am verifying this."

That was good enough for me. I turned and walked back to the edge of the forest.

A howling horde of demons spotted me and charged. It seemed that not all of them were engaged in the big battle. I stepped hastily back. "We have a problem."

"We do," Medea agreed. "Duban and I might hold off the demons, but that would not get us back to the Gate, and would attract attention. We do not know the outcome of the conflict of titans, but dare not presume its outcome. We need to get out of here on our own, swiftly."

It seemed I had another choice to make. "We'll brave the forest."

"Fool," Medea said, almost fondly.

Fool, Nylon and Nydea echoed, similarly.

Duban looked doubtful, but did not speak. He knew it was a difficult decision.

"If there's a way in, there must be a way out," I said, plunging ahead.

The path opened out, becoming a beautiful trail girt by foliage and flowers. It led to a pleasant glade.

And there, amazingly, were Jewel, Myrrh, and Nydea, together with Cerberus. Were they real, or illusions?

"How did you get here?" I asked.

"We were having a picnic," Jewel answered. "Then thought to take a walk in the pleasant grove. But we could not find our way out of it."

"All paths in the Lost Forest lead to the center," Medea said. "None lead out."

Then I was kissing Jewel, and Duban was hugging Myrrh. We were glad to be reunited. But we remained in a bad situation.

I oriented on Medea. "There has to be a way out. You would not have entered with us if you knew there was no escape."

"There may be," Medea said. "But it is complicated, and I do not know the route."

"But you know how to find it," Duban said.

"Perhaps. But that is not part of the truce."

She's bargaining, Nylon thought.

"What do you want?" I asked Medea impatiently.

"A deal for the real world outside Hades, at such time as we get there."

"What deal?"

Medea sighed. "You are not much for subtlety."

"I'm a man."

That certainly covers it, Nylon thought.

"You surely are. That is part of the point."

I was getting annoyed, but stifled it. "What deal?"

"I want to be your mistress."

"The Hades!" Jewel snapped.

"One of your concubines, then."

"What about Jason?" Jewel asked.

"He spurns me. My loyalty to him was foolish. I see that now. I want a man who is loyal to his wife."

That seemed nonsensical, but I saw Jewel considering. A man who was loyal to his wife should also be loyal to his concubines, so it did actually make sense. "What do you offer in return?"

"I believe I know of a person who can find a way out of the forest. Make the deal and I will summon her."

"Yet another concubine?" Jewel asked sharply. I could see that her patience with this sort of thing was limited.

"Not at all. Her interest is not of that nature."

"Done," Jewel said reluctantly. I knew she was desperate to get out of Hades and back home so she could have her baby in peace and comfort.

"Not yet," I said tersely. "Release my friend Sinbad. You can keep the Thief."

Medea looked regretful. "I was hoping you wouldn't think of that." She touched the ring on her hand. It dropped to the ground, unwinding, and landed as Sinbad.

"Beloved!" he cried, spying Nydea.

The two came together, kissing. Love had been restored.

Jewel caught my eye, nodding approval. I had managed to do something she appreciated.

"Now it's a deal," I said.

Medea turned to Cerberus. "Fetch Idrin. You can locate her telepathically. She will not be far away. No one is, here in the Lost Forest."

Cerberus bounded off, glad to be of service. Somehow the women had tamed him, and he evidently liked being treated like a pet.

"Who is Idrin?" I asked. "I have heard that name before."

"Indeed. So it seems you did not sleep entirely through your wife's narrations for the figurehead."

"The girl in my story!" Jewel exclaimed. "The one Idris Ifrit befriended. How can she be here?"

"This is the place of future folk as well as past folk. I knew she would be here."

Future folk? This was a fiction folk. Did it matter?

Cerberus bounded back. Astride two of his necks were two lovely young women. They dismounted and stood before us.

"We are so glad to meet you at last," the sultry one said to Jewel. "I am Idris Ifrit."

"I am Idrin," the other said, more shyly. "Thank you so much for creating me."

"But you're just a character in a story!" Jewel protested.

"I am so much more than that, thanks to you," Idrin said. "I owe you everything."

Jewel shook her head, not fully accepting this. So it was up to me to get to the point. "Can you show us the way out of here, Idrin?"

"Yes, but it is dangerous. It might be easier just to remain here."

"No," Jewel said firmly.

I knew that was that. My wife's firmness was another person's hard rock. "Can we trust her?" I asked Myrrh, whose telepathy was good for things like this.

"With your life," Myrrh said emphatically.

Was I missing something? This was a fictional person, animated here in Hades; she couldn't have much depth of character. Yet I trusted Myrrh's judgment. "Do it," I told Idrin.

The girl and the ifrit walked ahead of us, showing the way. They had similar figures, yet somehow the ifrit oozed sex appeal while the girl was merely a nice girl. Curious contrast.

Belatedly, I also noticed that we were not following a path, but rather were winding through crevices in the foliage. No path led out of the forest, but it seemed that there was after all a way.

We reached a kind of alley through the trees, where the ground was pressed flat and nothing grew. We paused.

"Here there be dragons," Idris said. "They threaten to consume any souls who venture this way."

Cerberus strode forward. "No, they have fire," Sinbad warned. "You can't get close enough to chomp them."

The big dog paused, accepting the caution.

"Duban?" I said. "Medea?"

Both of them stepped forward into the alley. Immediately the dragons charged from either direction, jetting fire. Duban held up his left hand, and the dragon on the left crashed into an invisible wall, painfully compacting its hot snoot. Medea held up her right hand and the dragon on the right encountered a scintillating curtain that electrified it; in fact for a moment its entire skeleton showed as a glowing internal framework. That was some shock!

We walked between the two defunct monsters and continued on our way as if nothing had happened. In due course we came to another alley. This one was patrolled by a giant ogre. It saw us and bared its yellow meat-chopper teeth. The women held Cerberus back. Duban and Medea stepped forth again, the ogre reached down, and received two water bombs in its ears. Or rather, acid bombs, because in moments its head melted. Disconcerted, the monster lumbered away, headless. Ogres were not smart; it would take it time to discover its loss.

"We work well together," Medea remarked to Duban. "Perhaps some day we will have more of a relationship."

"The Hades!" Jewel and Myrrh said together.

Medea merely smiled knowingly. I gritted my teeth.

Eventually we emerged from the forest and arrived at the outer wall. "How is it you knew the way out, when there is supposed to be no way out?" Jewel asked Idrin.

"No *path* out," Idris said.

"I'd rather not say," the girl said. "It's awkward."

"Oh, come on," Jewel said. "If you don't tell us, we shall have to find some way to repay you for your service to us."

"Oh, no, no need for that," the girl protested. "I would do anything for you. Anything at all. I owe everything to you."

I was curious too, so I let Jewel proceed in her relentless way. What was the mystery of this invented girl?

"I have greater freedom than other souls," Idrin finally explained, "because if I did not find the way out, there would be a paradox."

"Paradox!" Jewel said. "How can such a simple thing be that?"

"Because you are destined to continue your life in joy and fulfillment as Queen for a long time to come," Idrin said. "You could not do that if you did not escape Hades."

"Yes, of course. But how does this relate to you, when you're not even real?"

"I will become fully real in a few months, beyond Hades," Idrin said.

"A few months?"

The girl blushed. "When you birth me. I don't want to be born in Hades."

Jewel stared at her, speechless. That very seldom happened to my wife.

"Yes," Myrrh said softly. "Idrin is your daughter-to-be. That's why she is doing her utmost to help you."

Still wordless, Jewel hugged her, tears flowing. That, too, seldom happened to her.

Then Idrin disengaged and turned to me. I hugged her too, wordless and tearful. Beyond her I saw Medea, and I realized she had known. Instead of using it against me, she had honored our deal and used it on our behalf. It seemed she truly wanted our acceptance, apart from escape from Hades, just as Cerberus did.

"Mother, I must take the Key," Duban said. "It is a rare and potent artifact that could be dangerous near a baby. Lamprey is trusting me to safeguard it for him."

So that was what Lamprey had said to Duban. The boy was now a full magician, and could surely handle the dangerous artifact. Jewel handed over the Key.

Duban unlocked the Gate and we passed through. As we did, Idrin and Idris faded out. They were no longer in Hades. I wondered whether the ifrit would reappear after Idrin was born. I rather thought she would. After all, Jewel had made her too.

Somehow I knew already that Duban would now have the power to govern the Figurehead, and that we would have a safe sail home. I did not know whether Lamprey would defeat Hades, but was sure that Duban would find out when the time was appropriate.

I looked forward to being a father again. I liked Idrin already. As for Idris—I suspected she would be interested in being somebody's royal concubine. Things were looking very promising.

The End

Thank you for reading the Aladdin Trilogy. We hoped you enjoyed it.

Also available:

DRAGON ASSASSIN

by Piers Anthony and J.R. Rain
A mystery.
A fantasy land.
And one private eye who's life will never be the same again.

Available now!
Kindle * Kobo * Nook
Amazon UK * Apple * Smashwords
Paperback * Audio Book

Also available:

DOLFIN TAYLE

by Piers Anthony
and J.R. Rain

Dolfin Tayle is available at:
Kindle * Kobo * Nook
Amazon UK * Apple * Smashwords
Paperback * Audio Book

.

CHAPTER ONE

The killer is all around us, and I am afraid.

Around me, the sea is foaming and churning, and the dead are everywhere. Among the dead is my mother. I am confused and lost and hurt.

Earlier, something swept through the waters, something unseen, but felt by all. This unseen force gathered many of us up, along with other creatures of the deep. This thing, this sweeping thing, prevented us from surfacing, to breathe air.

I also got swept up into the force, got tangled into the invisible web. My mother was there, too, by my side. She fought frantically for me, tearing at the unseen material that kept us from surfacing. She used her great beak and teeth, and finally tore through what she called the netting.

But she could only tear a small opening, for this netting is nearly indestructible, and she was losing her strength. She needed to surface. All of us needed to surface. We needed to breathe. We were dying.

But there was only room for the smallest of us to escape.

My mother urged me through, and I listened to her, because I always listened to her, for my mother was known as the Seeker of Truth, and in her words was the truth, and I always listened to the Mother Seeker. Always, even when I did not want to. Always, even if I was tired or wanted to play with my friends.

Now my mother, the Seeker, urged me through the opening, holding this netting open with her strong jaws, speaking to me rapidly through clicks and chirps, our language of the deep. I did as I was told, and squeezed through the opening. She helped me through by nudging me with her bony beak. Our beaks aren't like bird beaks. No, they are long, bony protrusions that jut from our faces and allow us to snap at rapidly fleeing bass and mackerel, our favorite food.

Finally on the other side of this net, terrified, I listened as others began singing their death songs, and the ocean was filled with dying words and memories and voices and cries. I cried, too, and watched as others of our pod began floating silently up toward the surface, although they did not get very far. The netting held them in place, suspended in the water. Those whom I had once called uncle and aunt, those whom I had called friend and teacher, those who were kind and patient with me, those who were so wise to the ways of the deep, had finally quit fighting the net. And now they were floating.

The water, once alive with their fighting, filled with their haunting singing, slowly quieted and stilled.

"Hurry, ma," I said, zigzagging back and forth on the other side of the net. Above me, a human boat—a massive human boat, trawled slowly over the ocean, bouncing slightly on mild currents, its sleek and narrow shape a dark shadow above.

I saw that my mother was badly tangled. Her flukes and fens were bleeding as she struggled. She needed air. I needed air, too.

"I am stuck," she said. And as she spoke, I saw that she was fighting less and less. Blood wafted up from her many wounds as the net cut deep into her smooth hide. The more she fought, the more the net seemed to be holding her tighter and tighter, like a living thing. A great, evil thing. My mother, amazingly, smiled at me, although her face was growing a frightening shade of purple. She needed to breathe. She was dying. I needed to breathe, too. I would die unless I surfaced immediately.

"Please come with me, ma. Please."

"Live bravely, Azael," she said, calling me by my nickname.

"But I cannot live without you."

"You can do more than you ever dreamed. Go breathe. Go live."

"But—" But my breath was faltering. Darkness encroaches from the corners of my vision.

My mother spasmed violently; her blowhole quivered as it failed.

"I will not be far, my daughter. None of us will be. The sea is alive in you. Go now, girl. Now!"

And I did, turning up, thrusting with my tail and flukes, for I needed to breathe so very bad. From below my mother's death song reached me, and it was the most beautiful and horrible thing I had ever heard. I looked down once just as my mother's blowhole exploded open and she sucked in a great quantity of water. She shuddered convulsively...and then began floating.

I screamed and kicked hard and burst from the ocean like a flying beast. I released my air in a spray of water and inhaled deeply and landed with a massive splash.

But before I landed I saw clearly the markings on the ship. It was a white vessel with a large blue circle on its side, its hull, as my mother had taught me. The circle had the picture of a fish in it. Artwork, my mother had taught me. Humans were adept at art.

They were also adept at killing.

I would never forget that ship or the blue circle with the fish inside.

CHAPTER TWO

I watched in horror as the net was brought up to the surface, and with it the tangled bodies of those in my pod. I watched as my mother's lifeless form was pulled haltingly to the surface, for she was still very much entangled in the wicked webbing.

I followed her up, touching her, nuzzling her, drifting through the blood that surrounded her badly wounded body.

At the surface, as the sun shone high in the sky and seagulls circled, her body floated serenely in the wake of the ship, bouncing and bobbing. I floated with her, always careful of being ensnared in the webbing again. Others of our pod were there at the surface. All were dead. All floated lifeless, and the scene was too much for me to bear. I cried out and sang a song of deep sorrow. And as I sang, those humans on the ship turned and looked at me. Many watched me, holding their hands to shield their eyes. I saw one or two shake their heads, and then they went back to work, moving quickly, calling loudly to each other, doing whatever it is that they do on these ships.

Actually, I knew quite well what they did on this ship. They killed. And their netting was the instrument of death. Those creatures who did not need to breathe air were still alive, flopping wildly within the net, desperate and helpless, and even though only moments earlier my pod had been hunting them, I felt sorry for them, trapped as they were.

I continued to sing. I continued to nuzzle against my dead mother. The mackerel fought the netting furiously, twisting and angling their muscular bodies, damaging themselves. Great swaths of blood now drifted away from the netting, and I knew the sharks would be here soon, attracted by the blood. No doubt they were already on their way.

My mother was a beautiful creature. Long and elegant and sleek. Her eyes stared at me now, unseeing and lifeless, and I sang harder, my voice traveling far and wide.

Above, the humans worked quickly, hauling the net out of the water. I drifted on the currents, lifting and bobbing, staying close to my mother, but far enough away from the hateful netting.

And now my mother was moving, but not with life. No, she was being dragged over the surface of the ocean as the humans on board the ship gathered up the black net. As they took it in, I saw, they hauled great amounts of flopping mackerel from the ocean. They also hauled the bodies of my uncles and friends and those I had loved with all my heart.

My mother shifted on the currents, and then she was moving steadily toward the ship. She moved sideways. So unnatural. So painful to see. I did not want her to go up on that ship. I did not want her to leave the ocean. But I did not want to watch the sharks from the deep consume her, either.

I was torn and lost and full of pain. Still, I turned and dove under her lifeless body. I tore at the netting that held her in place, that cut into her body. But I could not tear it. How my mother had managed to do so, I did not know.

Still, she moved steadily toward the ship. And still I fought the netting, helpless.

"Leave her be, little one," said a voice from below. "You do not want to risk being caught yourself, correct?"

I did not know who spoke, but indeed the voice was right. Once or twice, as the net shifted and moved toward the floating ship, I had nearly become entangled myself. Through my tears and confusion, I looked down below and saw a very old seal.

"I do not want her to leave me," I said.

"Of course not, little one. But she would not want you to perish foolishly, either. Is your mother not the Seeker?"

I nodded.

"Then she has taught you that she will live on, yes? In spirit?"

I nodded again, and as I did so, I saw that I had drifted very close to the great ship. Men reached over the railing, hauling the netting up, using also what appeared to be a metal machine to aid them. My mother shifted. She was, I saw, slowly rising up out of the water.

"No!"

I was about to dash for her. I was about to plunge through the netting and tear her free. I was about to sink that whole blasted ship when the old seal reached out a fluke and wrapped it around me gently. "No, little one."

"But what will they do with her?"

He did not answer immediately, and together we watched as my mother, along with others from my pod, rose slowly out of the water, and flopped over the wall of the great ship...and disappeared from view.

"I do not know," said the old seal, and now he patted my back gently. "Come," he said. "The sharks will be here soon."

CHAPTER THREE

My pod was gone, and I was alone.

Well, not really alone. I was with the old seal, whose name was Kasmar. The ship had hauled its great net, bringing with it everyone and everything I had known and loved. Kasmar said it was better that we did not stay around, and I believed him, although I wanted to follow the ship. I wanted to follow it until they gave me back my mother.

"No, child," said Kasmar, as he gently nudged me away from the ship again, out toward the setting sun. "It is best we leave it be."

But we didn't leave, not yet. I had drifted up to the surface and lifted my head above the rolling waves, the wake left behind by the ship. As water gently splashed over me, as the sun shone down behind me, I watched the ship slip away over the ocean, hauling with it my pod.

My dead pod.

In a blink, in a span of moments, in a span shorter than it would take for me to consume milk from my mother, I was left alone in the ocean.

I sensed them coming from below. Actually, I heard them whispering, their low, guttural voices. Voices carry exceptionally well through water. I did not need to be close to them to hear them. The voices whispered of blood and hunger. The voices whispered of killing and destroying.

"Come," said Kasmar, he nudged me again, but this time harder. "We need to go."

I looked down, and far below I saw the white, torpedo shapes rising. Sharks, and not just any sharks. White sharks. Their whisperings grew louder.

A natural fear gripped me, and this time I heeded Kasmar's advice. He had already kicked off, and was looking back. I thrust my tail hard, and together Kasmar and I shot just beneath the ocean surface. I had been taught, long ago by my mother, to avoid splashing on the surface when the sharks were near, to keep from surfacing for air as long as possible, and so the two of us glided rapidly away from the scene of death, in the opposite direction. Far, far away from where they were taking my mother.

And when I couldn't last another moment without air, Kasmar and I surfaced together. He lifted his mouth and sucked in air, but I burst high above the waves, far higher than I had ever risen before, and as I twisted briefly in the air, the sunlight straight in my eyes, I let out a great, tormented cry.

I landed hard and not very smooth. Air burst from my blowhole, and together the old seal and I sped away. I knew one or two of the sharks had briefly given chase, but they let us go. After all, there was blood in the water to investigate.

Once or twice I waited for Kasmar to catch up to me, as the older seal could not swim quite as fast. But he was an excellent swimmer for his kind, and I was still young, and thus not as fast or swift as the older dolphins.

When we were many miles from the death scene and from the sharks, Kasmar and I finally slowed; it was then that I broke down and wept, my cries filling the ocean.

The old seal swam over to me and lay a flipper on my side, and we floated on the surface like that for a long, long time.

CHAPTER FOUR

At last growing hunger distracted me from my grief. I had to eat, or I would die, and that would waste the effort my mother had made to save me. She was gone, but I remained, and I had to do what I knew she wanted, and survive.

Kasmar understood, maybe before I did. "Let's go find some mackerel," he said.

We sniffed the water, orienting on that type of fish, and picked up the faint scent. I was glad for the seal's continued company; he was now my only link to my former life. Why he was helping me I was not sure, but I was not ready to question it.

Soon we located a small school of mackerel and dived in, as it were, catching the fish in our mouths, chewing them into bits, and swallowing the delicious fragments. Then, sated, we returned to the surface.

"What will you do now?" Kasmar inquired.

The question stumped me; I had no idea. My grief for my lost pod surged back overwhelmingly.

"Come visit with us," the seal suggested.

That surprised me, because seals and dolphins were only nodding acquaintances, foraging in similar places. But the notion appealed; I did not want to be alone. Now I had to ask: "Why are you helping me?"

"That's a bit complicated," he said. "Mainly it's because you're a child alone and you need some help, at least until you learn to manage on your own. But it is also that we seals have our own issues with the killer humans."

"Tell me," I said as we swam where he led. Maybe it would distract me from my misery.

"We seals, unlike dolphins, do some things on land. We have favored beaches for birthing and nurturing our babies, for one thing. We have cousins who make their families in very limited regions. And the humans come with clubs and bash the skulls of their babies, brutally killing them for their delicate fur. The carnage is awful, and the mothers mourn for weeks. We hate that, but can't stop the slaughter. I thought of that when I saw your pod about to get caught with the mackerel in the deadly net. I would have tried to warn you, but I could not catch up to you, and it was too late by the time I got close enough. All I could do was watch, and try to help if I could. You were the only survivor, so I came to you."

That made sense. "You seals suffer as we do," I said.

"We do."

Then I experienced a new emotion: the desire for vengeance. "I wish I could fling a big net over their cursed boat and haul it down into the sea until they all drowned, too."

Kasmar sighed. "I know I ought to tell you to avoid thoughts of revenge, to focus on positive things like lovely corals, the majesty of the mighty ocean, and personal survival. But I can't, because I feel as you do. I'd like to abolish the killer humans. The urge is pointless, because they have machines and weapons we can't touch, and just approaching them is dangerous. But still I wish for some retribution."

His confession was immensely reassuring. I was not alone in my feeling. And it gave me a mission: "I will find a way."

"Don't be foolish, little one. All you are likely to do is get yourself killed. You must learn to accept what you can't change, as I do. You don't have to like it; I don't. But you have to be realistic, or you won't survive."

"I'm too young to be realistic," I said rebelliously. "At least I must search for a way. That may give my life meaning."

"Maybe that will do," the seal agreed. "Just make sure that you don't convince yourself that you have the answer when you don't. Be realistic at least in your quest, so that if you ever do discover the way, you will know it is real and not foolish fancy."

That struck me as excellent advice, the kind my mother would have given me. "I will," I agreed. And the pain of my grief lessened somewhat, becoming slightly more manageable.

Kasmar took me to the seals, and they welcomed me. They were not my kind, but it was a comfort to be with them. Whether it was because I was so young, or that they shared Kasmar's outrage at what the humans did to their cousins, or some other reason I did not know. Maybe it was that Kasmar, as an elder seal, had influence to sway the others. But for now it sufficed.

ABOUT THE AUTHORS

Piers Anthony is one of the world's most prolific and popular authors. His fantasy Xanth novels have been read and loved by millions of readers around the world, and have been on the New York Times Best Seller list twenty-one times. Although Piers is mostly known for fantasy and science fiction, he has written several novels in other genres as well, including historical fiction, martial arts, and horror. Piers lives with his wife in a secluded woods hidden deep in Central Florida.

Please visit him at www.hipiers.com for a complete list of his fiction and non-fiction and to read his monthly newsletter.

———

J.R. Rain is an ex-private investigator who now writes full-time. He lives in a small house on a small island with his small dog, Sadie, who has more energy than Robin Williams.

Please visit him at www.jrrain.com.

Made in the USA
Middletown, DE
17 July 2021